TRIAL BY FIRE

It was probably going to be the last wagon train ever to go up the Oregon Trail, but right now the settlers were stranded in the middle of nowhere and they needed someone to get them safely to their destination. Sam Judge had captained a few trains in his day, but he had no hankering to relive those wild times. However, when they finally reached trail's end, he and his young partner, Matt Dury, found themselves facing a trial by fire!

Books by David Whitehead
in the Linford Western Library:

HELLER
STARPACKER

DAVID WHITEHEAD

TRIAL
BY FIRE

Complete and Unabridged

LINFORD
Leicester

First published in Great Britain in 1993 by
Robert Hale Limited
London

First Linford Edition
published June 1995
by arrangement with
Robert Hale Limited
London

British Library CIP Data

Whitehead, David
    Trial by fire.—Large print ed.—
Linford western library
I. Title II. Series
823.914 [F]

ISBN 0–7089–7707–3

Published by
F. A. Thorpe (Publishing) Ltd.
Anstey, Leicestershire

Set by Words & Graphics Ltd.
Anstey, Leicestershire
Printed and bound in Great Britain by
T. J. Press (Padstow) Ltd., Padstow, Cornwall

This book is printed on acid-free paper

For Jon Tuska, with thanks

1

I GUESS you could say the whole sorry business started the night Sam Judge shot Galveston Jones.

Earlier that evening, when he'd first shoved in through the batwing doors of Moynihan's Saloon and strode across to the bar with his two companions in tow, Jones had introduced himself by name, as if the name was supposed to mean something. In truth, of course, it meant very little, but that didn't stop Galveston Jones from thinking he was the most important man there, and behaving accordingly.

Standing six and one-half feet exactly, he was certainly the tallest of Moynihan's patrons. The tree-branch arms extending from his wide, sloping shoulders and the tree-trunk legs supporting his considerable weight probably made him the heaviest, too.

1

But build and bluster aside, Galveston Jones appeared to have just the one claim to fame; that of *being* Galveston Jones.

He dressed like an old-time mountain man. He wore his fringed and smeared buckskin shirt over plain hide pants that he tucked into knee-high moccasins. Slung diagonally across his fifty-inch chest was a bullet pouch and an ornately decorated possibles bag. He wore his weapons belt high; in back of it he carried a Green River skinning knife, and tucked butt-forward at the front sat two long-barrelled, heavy, single-action Walker .44s.

There was no doubt that wherever he went, Galveston Jones would attract attention, though not always for the right reasons. He was about forty summers old, with piggy blue eyes, a bulbous red nose and a shaggy, unkempt beard the same mouse-brown as the long hair that spilled from under his flat-brimmed Plainsman hat. His seamed skin had a cured, weathered quality and his teeth were yellow and gappy.

For all of that, though, he sure looked capable enough. In his time he doubtless really *had* done half the things he said he had. These days, however, being older, slower and running to fat, Galveston Jones preferred talking to doing, and he seemed to think the whole damn' world wanted nothing more than to hear his apparently endless fund of stories.

Until Jones had turned up, the atmosphere in Moynihan's combination saloon and eaterie had been cordial, if a mite rumbustious. A wagon train had dribbled in off the Oregon Trail earlier in the day, and the town — a hitherto quiet scattering of clapboard and oilpaper dwellings which had grown up around Fort Tierney, Nebraska — had come roaring to life. By the time early evening had rolled around and Sam Judge and Matt Dury had stepped in off the street to find a table at the back of the

3

place from which to order chicken pot pie and beer, Moynihan's was already packed to the rafters with local-men, off-duty soldiers, percentage girls and no-nothing Easterners in from the wagon train, making the most of what passed for civilisation before starting the next leg of their arduous trek to wherever.

Sam and Matt had been cooling their heels in the Cornhusker State following the bloody to-do with some *bronco* Apaches down in Mexico.[1] Their last vicious fight with those unsociable redmen had left Sam with a little piece of Apache lead in his left arm and the pair of them together with a sizeable collection of cuts and bruises and other assorted hurts.

Once their business down along the Arizona-Mexico line had been concluded, however, and a cavalry

---

[1] See *Law of the Gun*

officer reunited with the little girl he'd thought never to see again, the Texans had drifted north and east, allowing themselves to heal a bit before ending up here in Nebraska.

Sam was a tall, lean man forty-six years of age, with mild grey eyes, a long, slightly mournful face and short, thinning grey-black hair up beneath his round-crowned, buff coloured stetson. Up close he still showed the marks of a chequered career. He was missing the little finger of his right hand. There was some old scar tissue up around his eyes and nose, mementoes of a hundred desperate fist-fights. But just looking at him now, it was hard to believe that he had once been one of the west's most celebrated town-tamers, a man Ned Buntline himself had immortalised in more than a dozen dime novels as 'The Pistol Prince'.

Sam still handled the Remington .44 in the plain brown leather holster riding his right hip as good as he ever did, but his days as a celebrity were now pretty much over. After taming a town down in Colorado, place called Austin Springs, he'd stayed on as marshal, but his hunt to find the men who'd robbed the bank the previous summer and left two bodies behind 'em had reunited him with the man he now called partner, and pretty soon after that they'd gone on the drift together.[1]

Matt Dury was about half Sam's age, ruggedly handsome, with eyes that were a little darker than Sam's and a square jaw pitted by a dimple. A couple of inches short of the older man's six-two or -three, he nevertheless shared the same rangy, rawboned build and long, slightly mournful features. His hair was short, black and curly, and he was hell with the hide off with the Tranters he wore in his two-gun *buscadero* rig.

Back home in Brownwood, Texas, Matt had always looked upon Sam as a

---

[1] As told in *Hang 'em All*.

kind of adopted uncle. Before the War, Sam and his father had been partners in the Texas Rangers. But after Bob Dury died at Cemetery Ridge in '63, Sam had lit out to make a name for himself elsewhere. It was only fifteen years later that their paths had crossed again, and for the last half-year or so, they'd travelled the trail as partners.

Now they were intent on enjoying the relative luxury of home-cooked food and passable beer that Fort Tierney had to offer before continuing their aimless wanderings. 'Course, what they didn't know at the time was that Fate had other ideas.

Yep, it all started that night in Moynihan's Saloon, and but for a mangy old dog who should've known better, they'd have missed out on the entire affair altogether.

It worked out this way.

Galveston Jones, having regaled his unwilling audience with a string of stories specifically designed to show what a swell fellow he was, finally offered his farewells, turned and headed for the door. He had put away a considerable quantity of rotgut throughout the evening, story-telling being a thirsty business, and his stride on the way out was nowhere near as steady as it had been on the way in.

Having said that, the dog stretched out beside its owner, who was seated at a table near the batwings playing checkers, didn't help matters much.

Sam and Matt had noticed the dog on the way in, a shaggy black and white mongrel with liquid brown eyes and a twitching black nose that was constantly testing the air. The dog, like its master, was getting along in years and thickening out with age. Its master was a greybeard whose eyesight was poor, and that dog helped him get around, leading him patiently from the house he shared with his son and daughter-in-law to the saloon at which he liked to spend his days and evenings, playing checkers by touch. Once, Sam and Matt had even seen the dog get that old feller across the town's single, busy main street in one piece, too, avoiding all the horse and wagon traffic with the kind of intelligence you seldom saw in most humans.

Of course, the dog was not entirely a saint. In fact, it was as stubborn as any mule, and would never go around a man when that man could go around the dog. But most folks, knowing that the old man would have been finished long ago but for his loyal hound, were happy to let the dog stand its ground while they made the detour.

Galveston Jones, however, was not most folks. And from the way he stumbled across the dog, it didn't look as if he'd even seen the thing there in the first place.

Having met obstruction, he blundered forward and came up hard against the doorframe, all arms, legs and surprise. He was a mound of man, and there was not one jot of grace in his body. That was doubtless why one of the off-duty soldiers, standing by the staircase with one arm snaked around the waist of a pretty percenter, pointed at him and laughed, and a couple of his buddies pretty soon did likewise.

Galveston Jones, meanwhile, had spun around to see what had tripped him — or, to be strictly accurate about it, what he himself had tripped *over*. His expression was dark with anger and his scowl added deeper furrows to an already-lined visage.

"What 'n hell — ?"

He bit off as he noticed the dog, which had now climbed to its feet and was eyeing him balefully, for the first time. Realising then that the dog had caused him to flounder, and with half-drunken but good-natured laughter still ringing in his ears, Jones' lips curled up beneath his beard and he snarled, "Why, you sonofabitch — "

That's where it really started; when Galveston Jones drew back his right foot and kicked the dog. The animal hunched pitifully beneath the impact of the blow and yelped at the sudden, sharp pain in its left side. The force of the kick picked the critter up off the sawdusted boards and set it down again a foot or so away.

It went real quiet in Moynihan's then, for few men cared to see an animal abused in such a way, and at the table, hearing his dog cry out the way it did, the old man stiffened with his head cocked to one side, then twisted urgently in his chair.

"Jack? Jack, you all right, boy?"

Jones glared down at the squinting greybeard. "That your dog, mister?" he demanded.

Again the old man's head cocked to one side as he tried to distinguish the speaker. "Yeah. W-why?"

"Cause the next time it gets under my feet, I'm gonna shoot it. You hear me?"

The old man came up off his chair, lips twitching beneath his whiskers. He was dwarfed by Jones, who was at least thirty years his junior, too. "Now you see here," he began, reaching out to put a restraining palm on Jones' big chest.

"Aw, get offa me."

And that was when Jones made his second mistake, for he grabbed hold of the old-timer and shoved him back against the table, and the old man struck hard, stumbled and fell across it, spilling checkers every which-way.

It went *real* quiet in the saloon then, but it was a silence that didn't last long; almost at once it was broken by a low, ominous growling as the dog, Jack, went down low before the man who'd just attacked his master, baring his teeth as the rumble came deep and dangerous up out of his guts.

Any reasonable man would've called it a day right there and then. But Galveston Jones wasn't a reasonable man. Instead, he reached for one of the Colts at his belt and his intention was clear; he figured to go ahead and shoot the dog anyway.

One of the off-duty soldiers over by the staircase quickly stepped forward.

He was a young man, red-faced from an evening's merry-making but earnest in his desire to stop this little altercation from going any further.

"Now hold up there, mister," he began, reaching around to unbutton his own sidearm.

Galveston Jones turned to face him. He had an evil temper even when sober. Now, his piggy blue eyes flared with fresh anger, and very deliberately he drew his left-side .44, thumbed back the hammer and shot the soldier in the chest.

A couple of women screamed. There came a collective gasp from the assembled men. The young soldier back-pedalled, reaching now for the red hole in his shirt-front, lost his balance and fell over.

There was a moment then when the whole world held its breath. Then pandemonium broke out in Moynihan's Saloon as one of the soldier's friends pulled his Cavalry Colt free of leather and Jones' two big buddies also groped for their handguns.

Townsfolk and percentage girls threw themselves to the floor and under tables. Suddenly the entire affair had gotten out of hand. The soldier got off one shot. It missed by a mile. One of Jones' companions — big, clad in buckskin, clean-shaven but for a steerhorn moustache — returned fire with a big old Navy Starr, catching the fellow high in one shoulder.

As the soldier spun around and away, the old dog threw itself at Jones' thick legs. With a roar he kicked it away, fired his gun wildly into the crowd just for the hell of it, then switched his sights to the now-cowering dog as its master yelled, "Jack! Jack!"

Jones was just thumbing back the hammer again when Sam Judge came up out of his chair at the back of the place with his Remington .44 extended to arm's-length. "That's enough of that, Jones!" he snapped. "Now cool that iron or so help me, I'll cool you!"

Jones' puffy little lamps twitched up

in their sockets and focused on the tall, lean stranger in the unremarkable range-wear, but in his fiery, liquored-up state he only saw one more target.

The Walker moved in his fist, shifting aim. Sam saw it, saw that Jones wasn't about to cool anything, snap-aimed at the big sonofabuck and shot him in the right breast.

Jones staggered under the impact of the slug, but he didn't go down the way a normal man would. His attention sharpened on Sam just as that of his trigger-happy friends did likewise, and Matt Dury came around his partner, face expressionless but Tranters blazing in his hands as he cut them down with lethal efficiency.

For frenzied moments the smoky air quivered to the thunder of gunfire. As his companions twisted and spun under the sledgehammer force of Matt's bullets, discharging their own weapons into the tin ceiling or the sawdusted floor, Jones roared something that only he could understand and brought his

15

Walker Colt up yet again.

Not that Sam was having any of that. Methodically, he thumbed back the hammer and shot Jones again, and as Jones took a wide, uncertain pace backwards, he let him have one more slug, and as that struck, Jones flew rearward, slammed into the batwings and collapsed on the boards outside.

Into the silence came the moaning of the wounded. Over his shoulder, Sam told the ruddy-faced bartender whom he took to be Moynihan to go fetch the doctor. The marshal, he figured, was probably already on his way. He shoved his gun back into leather and quickly strode to the front of the saloon to inspect the damage.

He could feel the stunned shock of the people watching him. Some of the women were sobbing. Many of the men were pale-faced and trembling. He paused beside the soldiers at the foot of the staircase. One of them was dead, the other now being tended by his friends.

Next, he ran a critical eye over Jones' two partners. Matt had killed the feller with the steerhorn moustache outright. The other one was rolling around on the floor, hugging himself.

After peering outside to make sure that Jones was also out of it, Sam turned back to face the room. Order was slowly returning to the chaotic watering-hole. Jones' wild shot had struck a girl at the back of the crowd. A couple of people were trying to stop the bleeding in her stomach, but from where he was standing, it looked hopeless.

A movement to his left caught his eye and he reached down to help the myopic old man to his feet. Through the coarse wool of his shirt Sam felt the old fellow shaking.

"All right, old son, it's all right now."

"My dog," the old-timer said fretfully. "Is he — ?"

"He's right here." Sam guided the man's liver-spotted right hand down to the dog's head. As soon as he made contact, the old-timer relaxed a little and rubbed the dog's ears. "Bless you, friend," he said quietly.

Sam patted him on the shoulder just as Matt came over. The younger man's face was grim, for he took just about as much pleasure from killing as did his companion.

"You all right?" he asked.

Sam started to reload. "Sure. You?"

"Nary a scratch. Not like that poor kid." Matt indicated the wounded percentage girl, who had just died.

"Damn."

Things got a little more organised when the army surgeon and his orderly arrived from the nearby outpost, by which time the local part-time constable had also turned up and was trying to make sense out of all that had happened. It was a pretty messy business, of course. These things were rarely anything but. Fortunately for those involved, however, it was also pretty straightforward. In the circumstances, Sam had done right to cut the wild man down as fast as he had, and neither were his two knavish companions much of a loss.

But as the man once said, for every action, there's a reaction. Just throw a pebble into a lake, and watch the ripples it throws back out in ever-widening circles. Well, that's how it was with the killing of Galveston Jones. It had what you might call *repercussions*.

By noon of the following day, Sam and Matt had decided to shake the dust of Fort Tierney from their heels. The unpleasantness down at Moynihan's place had already given them a degree of notoriety they had no wish to acquire, and it had soured what little peace and anonymity they had found in the town.

But like I said; Fate had *other* ideas.

No sooner had they settled their bill at the livery stable at the west end of town and started to rig out their horses for travelling, than two shadows fell across the ground and they turned to find themselves being regarded by an ill-matched couple of newcomers.

The man was about fifty or so, short, stout, round-faced, clean-shaven, with cold blue eyes. He took his hat off as he peered around the place through flimsy-looking wire-framed spectacles. He was bald but for a fringe of closely-cropped white hair. He wore a suit of rusty black broadcloth that bore all the usual stains of travel. His once-white shirt was now creased and frayed, and his black string tie looked equally abused.

His companion was something else entirely. She was tall, and her hourglass frame was encased in a two-piece outfit of powder blue, a short jacket worn over a frilly white blouse, and split riding skirt. Her hair was thick and coppery, piled up in an appealing series of curls and swirls. She wore a jaunty little hat atop it.

It was her face that attracted Sam most of all, however. Through the gloom of the stable, it seemed to shimmer. She returned his look through cool brown eyes. She had a kind of haughty, regal bearing, a very small, very straight nose, heart-shaped lips, the merest hint of colour on her cheekbones. She was about forty or so, but almighty well preserved on it.

The odd couple came across to the Texans, footsteps loud and intrusive on the packed-earth floor, and hovered there with the little man turning his hat in his smooth, very clean hands. After a while he said, "Mr Judge? Mr Samuel Judge?"

Sam eyed them both a little closer. Nope, he didn't know them from anyplace. He nodded. "I'm Judge. Help you?"

A smile twitched awkwardly across the little man's pale lips. "I think so, sir. The clerk at your hotel said we would find you here."

"Did he, now?"

There was a moment of silence then, until the little man stirred himself back into action. "Uh, please, allow me to introduce us. My companion here is Mrs Charlotte Minto. I am Reverend Berry, Elijah Berry." The preacher's face clouded up then. "We are here in connection with the . . . ah . . . killing of Galveston Jones, last night."

Sam let loose a brief smile of his own. "Well, meanin' no offence, reverend, but if you're here to try savin' our souls, you're a little late."

"We are here for no such thing," the woman, Mrs Minto, cut in. She had a strong, deep voice that was at once both authoritative and feminine. "We came to find you to see what you intended to do about it."

Now Sam frowned. "Do about it? Ma'am, I've already done it. I plugged 'im. And you can wipe that look of disapproval off your face. I took no pleasure from the deed, but it had to be done."

"Oh, I don't dispute that for one moment," she replied. "From my own experience, I found Mr Jones and his cohorts to be eminently disagreeable, but I wonder, sir, whether you stopped to spare a thought for the men, women and children in Mr Jones' care before you dispensed your rough-and-ready brand of justice?"

Sam and Matt exchanged a glance. Matt, as thoroughly puzzled as his partner but just a tad more diplomatic, said, "Excuse me, ma'am, but I think you'd better explain just what it is you stopped by to say."

It was the reverend who replied. "We have come to ask what you intend to do to salvage this very unfortunate situation, Mr Judge. Need I impress upon you, sir, that we were entirely dependent upon Mr Jones getting us safely through to our destination?"

Narrowing his eyes, Sam hazarded a guess. "You're with that wagon train that pulled in yesterday?"

"Yes, sir."

"An' Galveston Jones . . . ?"

"Galveston Jones was our wagon-master," said Charlotte Minto. "A

23

disagreeable man, as I have said, but a guide of some skill and intelligence."

Now Sam was starting to see it all clearly. "An' you're here to find out what *I'm* figurin' to do about gettin' you through to wherever it is you're goin'?"

"Indeed we are, Mr Judge."

"Well, I'm sorry, but there's nothin' I can do for you but suggest you find yourselves another guide."

"You don't consider yourself at all responsible for the predicament into which you have thrown one hundred and fifty people?" asked the woman, anger lighting her brown eyes appealingly.

"Why should I?" Sam replied bluntly. "I didn't want to kill your Mr Jones, ma'am, but by his foolish actions he brought that misfortune on himself, an' if that leaves you folks in a fix, well, I'm sorry, but it's nothin' to do with me."

"Mr Judge," said Reverend Berry. "Might I ask you a question?"

"I'd as soon you didn't."

Ignoring the response, Berry said, "I'm curious, sir, as to why you got involved in that shooting last night at all. I have made enquiries. The trouble had nothing whatever to do with you: you were, I believe, seated at the far end of the saloon. So why did you choose to become involved?"

Until now, Sam had not even thought to question that himself. He guessed he'd been a lawman so long that it just came naturally. "Jones was drunk," he said after a moment. "He went kill-crazy. *Someone* had to put him down."

"But surely you could have left that to someone else?"

"There *was* no-one else; leastways, no-one who could've put him down as fast."

Reverend Berry positively beamed. "Then surely, sir, you can see *our* predicament. *We* have nobody else — only *you*, Mr Judge; the very man who put us in this rather unfortunate position in the first place."

Sam snorted. "I'm sorry, reverend,

but it won't work. I killed Jones, sure, but that doesn't automatically make me responsible for *you*."

"But Mr Judge . . . it's not as if we are being unreasonable. I am familiar with your reputation. I know you have captained wagon trains before."

"Heck, reverend, that was twenty years ago!"

"It's not even as if we aren't prepared to pay you for your trouble," Mrs Minto interjected. "Where is your sense of honour, sir?"

"Ma'am, this's got nothin' to do with money or honour or responsibility. If you want me to lay it out plain, all right, I will. I need to wet-nurse your hundred and fifty Easterners like I need a hole in the head. That plain enough for you? I don't want the job, and there's not one good reason in the world why I should have to take it." He drew in a calming breath. "Now, where're you headed?"

"To Spruce Valley," Berry said, his eyes lighting up as he voiced the name.

"It's up in the Rocky Mountains, sir, and positively the closest place to almighty Zion on the face of this continent."

"Well, you keep trendin' west for another couple hundred miles or so an' you ought to reach it just fine."

The preacher eyed him tight-lipped. After a pause he said, "And that is your last word on the matter?"

"No; my last words are 'Good Luck'."

"Very well," Charlotte Minto said in a low, angry voice. "Very well, Mr Judge. Let us take up no more of your valuable time. But let me also tell you this; that we Easterners might prove to be hardier than you give us credit for. And though our journey will be far more dangerous for want of an experienced guide, though we may suffer harder and perhaps lose more of our number on the trail, we will overcome every adversity, sir, and become the stronger for it!"

She doubtless would have gone on

and made a full-blown speech of it, but at that moment there came a rustling of straw from somewhere back in one of the stalls and Charlotte Minto, hardy pioneer, leapt back with a startled yelp, her brown eyes wide and her heart-shaped lips describing a perfect *O*.

"My goodness! Rats!"

Sam could not help but shake his head in despair. "Not rats, ma'am," he said, bending to scoop up an overweight tan-and-white Abyssinian cat with large sea-green eyes. "*Cats. One* cat, to be precise." As he deftly slipped the animal into his right-side saddlebag, he said, "But don't fret. She's harmless. Been with me nigh-on four years now. I call her Mitzi, after a lady I once knew in Black Rock, Nevada."

But the woman, feeling foolish as hell, didn't care to hear the cat's history. Turning on her heel, she said, "Come along, Reverend Berry! Let us detain these men no longer!"

As they hustled out, Sam shook his head some more and said, "Easterners!"

2

AS the Texans led their horses out onto the street, they spotted a weary-looking detachment of soldiers walking their mounts into town from the west. The officer at the head of the small column was a stern-faced fellow in his mid-twenties, clean-shaven but for a curling moustache the colour of strong tobacco. The plain sleeves of his greatcoat (for the spring afternoon still held some of the sharpness of the winter just gone) indicated his rank; that of a second lieutenant. The men behind him rode slump-shouldered and easy in their equipment-heavy McClellan saddles, each one young and rawboned.

A civilian up on the opposite boardwalk hailed the officer. Looking that way, Sam and Matt recognised Harvey Mailer, the part-time constable.

The lieutenant raised a hand to the brim of his campaign hat and swung his horse towards him. A brief discussion followed, while Sam and Matt checked their rigs one last time and Mitzi surveyed their surroundings from her vantage point in Sam's saddlebag. Then the second lieutenant straightened back up and led his patrol on towards the outpost which had given the town its name, a rough-hewn compound two or three hundred yards further east, near to which were stalled the forty or so wagons comprising Reverend Berry's west-bound train.

It was then that Mailer noticed the men from Texas, and raised his hand in greeting as he came down off the boards and crossed the street to brace them. He was a tall, loose-limbed man of an age with Sam, with a round, hard-skinned face and gentle brown eyes. He wore the badge pinned to his vest lapel primarily as a means of supplementing the meagre income he made as a handyman, but that didn't mean to say he took his law duties lightly. Now, as he came level with them, he nodded briskly.

"Afternoon. You fellers goin' someplace?"

"Leavin'," Sam replied. "Headed east."

"That's funny. I figured you'd be headin' west."

"Oh? Why?"

Mailer hooked a thumb up the street. "I jus' seen that preacher-man come out of the livery, suspicioned he'd been after you to lead his wagon train into the Rockies."

"Well, you're right about that. He did try, him an' that Mrs Minto both, but we declined the invitation."

"Too bad. The way I hear it, they've spent most of the mornin' up at the fort, tryin' to scare up a replacement for Galveston Jones."

"Without success, obviously," Matt remarked.

Mailer shrugged. "You jus' don't find wagon-masters this far northwest, not good 'uns, I mean, ones as know their business. 'Part from anythin' else, there's not the demand there was thirty years ago."

That was certainly true. These days, folks used the Oregon Trail mostly to run cattle or sheep down from the east, and what travellers there still were would use it even less when the Oregon Short Line railroad came into service.

The constable rubbed his palms together. "Say, buy you fellers a drink afore you go?"

"Sure. Thanks."

They crossed back over toward Moynihan's place, tied up at the rack outside and clattered in through the batwings. It was a little warmer inside the saloon, and since the place was now catering only to a sparse lunchtime trade, not half as crowded as it had been the previous evening. The blood around the doorway had been scrubbed away, Sam noted as they went in, and fresh sawdust had been scattered. Now the place smelled of carbolic, and in a way that smell was worse than the stench it was meant to disguise.

Mailer told the bartender to set up three whiskies, then propped himself up against the mahogany counter. "Well, here's to you," he said.

They drank.

"I hear you've captained a train or two in your time, Judge," the lawman remarked casually as the whiskey settled in their bellies.

A smile touched Sam's thin lips. "You hear a lot of things around here, marshal."

"All part of the job."

"I guess." He paused, remembering. "Sure, I captained a few. But things were different then, those times were wilder. We had the Indians to contend with, for one thing. Arapaho, Cheyenne, Sioux. You know, sometimes I figure I've traded shots with just about every tribe there is to name."

"Oh, they're still out there, Judge."

"But well an' truly pacified."

Mailer shrugged. "It suits them to let us believe that. Still, Indians' not the only problem a man has to face on the Trail. You see that patrol jus' come in a while back? They been out after Django Reilly."

Matt set his glass down. "Who the hell's Django Reilly?"

"Aw, some bloody-hungry Mexican-Irishman up from the southwest, runs a gang of like-minded bravos. You haven't heard of him, then?"

"It's been a while since I packed a badge," Sam explained. "Guess we're kind of behind the times."

"He robbed a mess o' banks and trains down in Arizona and New Mexico," Mailer explained. "When he made things too hot for himself down there, he came north and started preyin' on folks travellin' the Trail. Been at it for four, five months now."

"The soldier-boys had no luck?" Matt prompted.

Mailer snorted and signalled for

refills all around. "Department of the Platte's had patrols out from Alcove Springs to Independence Rock, but it's jus' too much country to cover."

"Besides which," Sam pointed out, "the army's got a way of movin' that tells a man exactly where it's at long before it even gets close."

"Ezzackly," Mailer agreed with a nod.

"Not that I'm condemnin' the army," Sam added, rubbing at his still-sore left arm, where the surgeon at Camp Randall, Arizona Territory, had taken that Apache bullet out of him with considerable skill.

They spent the next twenty minutes shooting the breeze the way most men do, discussing and offering opinions on all manner of current topics, from the state's recent dramatic increase in corn production to whether or not the mild mannered Manuel Gonzales was really going to be the president Mexico needed. Eventually the steadily-increasing rattle and creak of approaching wagons made them turn their attention to the street beyond the batwings.

They were just in time to see the first of them trundle past, a canvas-covered prairie schooner with plain plank sides and bright red wheels, the whole three or four-ton structure being hauled by six massive oxen leaning into three hickory yokes. Up on the seat sat a pale-looking woman in a poke bonnet and dusty black dress. Walking beside the team with a whip in his hand was Reverend Berry.

Sam, Matt and the constable were drawn across the saloon to witness the spectacle. At the table near the door, the old man who liked to play checkers by touch was listening to the sounds now filling the street, and his old mongrel, Jack, sniffed at Sam's pants-leg as he went past, and wagged his tail.

The men stepped out onto the porch. All the way up and down both sides of the street, the boardwalks were lined with townsfolk who had come out to watch the procession.

And procession it certainly was, Sam thought as he fished out one of his noxious three-for-a-dime cigars and lit up; forty Conestoga wagons, drawn by oxen or thick bodied plough-horses; here and there some plodding milkcows or goats; a few bearded men on horseback, others striding along beside their team-animals, goading them on with whips or quirts. Sam watched the bunching of the oxens' muscles as a thin cloud of dust began to rise beneath the iron-tyred wheels. He looked into the faces of the men, women and children. He did not expect to see smiles. This wasn't an adventure, not for these folks, it was sheer hard toil. The people looked worn-down, ill-used, but determined.

"Settlers," he remarked sourly to no-one in particular. "Just look at 'em. Green as moss. Maybe now you can see why I didn't care much for the job o' changin' their diapers from here till they get wherever they're goin', marshal."

"Easterners an' emigrants, the way I hear it," Mailer said, raising his voice to be heard above all the racket. "Folks from New York and Pennsylvania mostly, but a sizeable number of Germans, Eyetalians, Swedes and Irish, too."

"Bound for a place called Spruce Valley," Matt put in.

Mailer nodded. "So I heard."

Some more wagons swayed and jounced by, canvas awnings quivering to the motion, grease buckets swaying from rear axles. It was about then that Sam got the feeling he was being watched, and when he switched his attention down the street a-ways to the next wagon in line, he saw Charlotte Minto glaring at him from up on the high seat, still rigged smartly in powder blue, but handling her four-horse team like a veteran.

There was a girl up on the seat beside her, perhaps seventeen or eighteen, and she shared the older woman's clear, ivory complexion and lustrous red hair, though her own was cut to shoulder length. Her eyes were the same clear blue as the Nebraska sky above. She wore a checked shirt beneath her pea jacket, jeans and boots, though the clothes detracted little from her obvious femininity.

Sam switched his attention back to Mrs Minto, then. He found the woman still staring at him. As she drew level, he reached up and touched his hat-brim in greeting. Then she was gone, her wagon tracing the rutted street west, away from Fort Tierney, taking a similar course to the wagons ahead as they turned slowly southwest and began to follow the contortions of the South Platte River.

"Well, I'll not detain you," Harvey Mailer said at last. "I got chores to do, an' I daresay you'll be wantin' to make tracks yourselves."

"That we do, marshal," Sam nodded.

Mailer extended his hand. "All the

luck to you, then, Judge. You too, Dury. Ah . . . Dury?"

Matt peeled his dark grey eyes away from the westward wagons. "Uh . . . yeah. Be seein' you, Mailer."

As the lawman ambled away, Sam eyed his young companion with mild amusement. Taking the cigar from his mouth, he blew smoke and said, "You seem a mite preoccupied, boy."

Matt shrugged. "Oh, it's nothin'."

"You sure?" Sam stepped down into the street and unhitched the somewhat gnarled old strawberry roan he had long ago christened Charlie. "Seems to me you was all right till you caught sight of that girl who was sittin' up there alongside Mrs Minto."

Matt laughed. "Aw hell, don't fix to marry me off *just* yet, mama." He also came down to untie his clean-limbed cow-pony. "Still, she *was* awful pretty, wasn't she? Did you see the blue of her eyes, Sam?

Sam chuckled. "Sure, I saw."

They swung across leather and

angled their animals east, walking them past a seemingly endless flow of wagons with Mitzi still watching their surroundings with curiosity from under the saddlebag flap.

The whiskey had mellowed Sam. It always felt good to be moving on, too. He'd packed a badge in Austin Springs for a whole mess of years, grown old there and set in his ways. But as soon as he'd rediscovered the world beyond the town's limits, his life had regained some of its old bite.

He eyed the folks rattling past, meeting their cold stares impassively. Did they know they had him to thank for setting them adrift without a guide? Had that blasted Minto woman spread the word? Or was it simply that these poor dumb settlers had been washed out, drained of life and hope by the hardships of the half-continent they'd already travelled?

He watched them pass by, that kaleidoscope of faces, all serious, listless, without colour. He could only hope that when they finally made it to Spruce Valley, they'd consider the whole trip worthwhile.

The town fell behind them and the trail opened out ahead. To their left stood the compound and a large notice pinned to a board beside the roadway, which said:

GOVERNOR'S PROCLAMATION!

WHEREAS the route known as the Oregon Trail has recently become the stamping ground of the outlaw DJANGO REILLY, and that the depredations of said outlaw have resulted in the WANTON MURDER of AT LEAST 9 innocent travellers, the Governor of this Great State of Nebraska does hereby offer a reward of FIVE HUNDRED DOLLARS for the arrest or extermination of the said Django Reilly and a further TWO HUNDRED DOLLARS for each of his associates, believed to number one dozen."

Reilly is described as about 6 feet in height, 28 years of age, dark complexion, black hair, brown eyes, erect form.

Sam did a little figuring and then whistled low in appreciation. "Whoo-boy! The governor must want Reilly awful bad. You know how much that reward comes out to?"

"Just under three thousand dollars," Matt replied. He glanced over at the other man. "Maybe we ought to keep our eyes peeled."

"Maybe we should at that," Sam agreed, rubbing his chin. Although he'd never been one to seek bounty, three thousand dollars or thereabouts was a powerful tempter. And though he hated to admit it, even to himself, he kind of favoured the idea of tangling with such a notorious varmint for much the same reason he'd punctured Galveston Jones; because he'd been a lawman for so much of his life that it ran in his blood now, was a part of him that came as naturally as breathing.

"Course . . . " Matt began as they nudged their mounts back to a walk.

"Yeah?"

"Well, I was jus' thinkin'. Man figures to catch a rat like this here Django Reilly, he'd stand a whole lot better chance if he had decent bait."

Sam tossed his cigar-stub away. "Like that wagon train back yonder, you mean?"

Matt shrugged. "Forty wagons, Sam. Hundred-fifty people. Rich pickin's for someone like this Reilly. An' he's bound to've heard it's on its way."

Sam saw the logic to that. "You figure we should maybe tag along with 'em after all, then?"

"It's a thought."

"An' that 'thought' wouldn't have nothin' to do with a certain young girl with sweet blue eyes, I suppose?"

Matt laughed. "Never entered my mind."

Sam thought it over. He'd done this

line of work before, it was true. But that made it all the more crazy for him to do it again. Still . . . Once more he saw those lifeless faces in his mind. Those Easterners could sure use some help if they were going to make it through to Spruce Valley in one piece. Especially if this Django Reilly *did* come a-callin'. Besides which, he'd seen no sign of a *Mr* Minto around Charlotte Minto's wagon, and as feisty as she was, she sure was handsome with it.

"All right," he said at length, turning his roan back toward the west. "If they'll still have us, I don't guess we've got all that much to lose."

He kicked the horse to a gallop, and Matt matched him all the way back to the head of the distant column.

★ ★ ★

"Gentlemen," Reverend Berry said piously, "you will not regret this decision, I can promise you. You are undertaking the Lord's work here, leading us through to our promised land in the distant mountains. *I* thank you, sirs. These *people* thank you. But you will surely receive your greatest reward when you come to enter the Kingdom of Heaven."

Sam and Matt exchanged a glance. It hadn't taken long to catch the wagon train up. They'd ridden back through town and followed the single street out onto the southwest trail. The country out this way was flat and verdant. The South Platte River flowed sluggishly away to their right. Ahead, the plains stretched out green and prolific, good cattle-grazing country. Here and there, little patches of winter snow still clung to the ground, too stubborn to soften and disperse beneath the admittedly-weak spring sun. In the hazy distance, timber-thick hills rose in a blue-green spill, their jagged tips hidden beneath low cloud.

The wagon train had been winding a ragged course across the land. Even from this distance Sam could see they needed some discipline. There was too much space between one wagon and the next, and some of them had already broken formation; they'd have to be tightened up and taught how to follow each other in a half-way orderly fashion.

Overtaking the column wasn't difficult. They'd swung out a way and cantered along the line, headed for Reverend Berry's wagon, creaking along at a sedate pace up front, and pretty soon after that the reverend, surprise and puzzlement clear on his round, smooth face, had yelled the order to halt, and as the cry went back down the line, Sam had nodded a greeting and asked the preacher if he was still looking for a wagon-master.

"Why, of course we are, sir! We had no luck at all trying to hire one at Fort Tierney, and had decided to make a stab at going it alone."

"Well, if the offer's still open . . . "

It was.

"Then it looks like you just hired yourself two guides, reverend."

The preacher's face lit up. But before he could go any further than promising them a place in heaven in return for their services, Sam got down to cases.

"Now, we'll get this train of yours into some kind of order before we go any further, if you please. Matt, I'd be obliged if you'd ride back down the line and tell these good folks to close ranks a tad, an' try to keep in track."

"Yo!"

"An' no dallyin' with Little Miss Blue Eyes, you hear me?"

Matt grinned and nodded. "*Yo!*" He wheeled his pony and started back down the stalled column, calling orders and instructions and indicating with wide sweeps of his free hand exactly what he wanted the settlers to do.

"You have a map to your destination, reverend?" asked Sam.

"Why yes, right here . . . " Berry turned to the woman up on the high seat. "Jessica?" Wordlessly she passed down a folded map. As the sky-pilot handed it up to Sam he thought to make introductions. "My sister Jessica, Mr Judge."

Sam nodded. "Pleased to know you, ma'am." The woman barely inclined her head in reply.

The man from Texas unfolded the map and studied it a moment. "Your people are all fit enough to travel, I suppose?" he asked absently.

"They are."

"No signs of disease at all? Typhoid, dysentery, scarlet fever, malaria — "

"They are not the sickly weaklings you would believe them to be, Mr Judge. And in any case, we have two doctors among our number."

"You got any hunters out?"

Berry frowned. "Hunters?"

"Men chasin' up food?"

"Oh. No. I . . . Mr Jones took care of all that."

"Well, Mr Jones isn't with us any more," Sam reminded him, looking up at last. "An' like it or not, reverend, your people still have to eat." He sighed. "All right. We'll spell the animals in a couple of hours. When we do, I want you to find me the best riflemen you can."

"Very well."

"I notice you didn't have any rear guards out, either."

"Should I have?"

"It sure wouldn't do any harm. A few men out front wouldn't go amiss, either. We'll sort that out when we take that breather, too."

He glanced at the map one more time. When he figured he had his bearings, he refolded it and stuffed it into his saddlebag, next to Mitzi. "All right, reverend. Let's get movin'. We can discuss our terms of employment later tonight."

"As you wish, sir."

Turning his roan to the south and west, Sam swung his right arm in a high overhead arc. "*Ho!*"

The roan set off at a trot.

The wagon train rolled slowly out behind it.

★ ★ ★

It required the patience of a saint to make this kind of trek, for it was a slow, slow business as the mile-long caravan crawled on across the endless, lonely prairie. It took patience, determination and a certain kind of tenacity, and when the occasion demanded it, Sam had plenty of it all. Even so, the feeling stayed with him for the rest of the day that he'd somehow shot himself in the foot by taking this job on.

He hadn't wanted it. Who would? Still, he might just as well go ahead and admit to himself that he'd felt sorry for these hard-luck emigrants. Apart from the chance he and Matt might get to lock horns with Django Reilly and pick up some useful spending money if things went according to plan, he really figured they could use the help he had to offer.

Out ahead of the column, he snorted and shook his head. He must be getting soft in his old-age.

As the afternoon wore on, he rode back along the line to make sure the wagons were keeping tight. There were still a few stragglers, but the majority were trying mightily to do as they'd been told.

Around the middle of the afternoon he called the promised halt. Wearily, working more by habit than anything else, the would-be settlers turned their oxen loose without removing their yokes and saw to the remainder of their animals before considering their own comfort.

Sam, having dismounted, seen to the comfort of his roan and let Mitzi down to wander off on her own, surveyed their surroundings. He could think of worse country to have to cross. The military road had made the travelling easier than he'd expected, and there was no shortage of wood, water or grass. Unless he was mistaken, the most difficult stage of the journey would come when they began to ascend the mountains.

Matt rode in and cooled his saddle. He had spent most of the afternoon keeping the wagons on track and helping those folks who had run into difficulties. Now, as he loosened his animal's cinch and removed the bit from its mouth so that it could graze, Sam said, "Well?"

Matt looked up at him from under a frown. "Well, what?"

Sam took out a cigar. "What's her name an' who is she?"

Matt's grin spread slowly. "Her name's Rachel and she's Mrs Minto's daughter."

"Well, I'll say one thing for you, boy. You sure don't believe in wastin' time." Sam struck a match and puffed the cigar to life. "So her name's Rachel, huh?" he remarked with studied casualness. "An' what's her papa think to you pesterin' his little girl all the time?"

Matt said, "Her papa's dead. Died about two years ago — " Suddenly he broke off. "Why, you sly old fox! Interested in her mama, are you?"

"I never said that . . . "

Reverend Berry came across then, with about fifteen men of all shapes and sizes in tow, the youngest of them in his late teens, the oldest crowding fifty. "Ah, Mr Judge. And Mr Dury," the preacher said in greeting. "Good afternoon to you, sirs. As you can see, I've found the men you requested."

Sam nodded. "Thanks." He eyed them sternly. Three of them had the dark, Latin features of Italians. One had a Prussian look about him. The rest appeared to all be American. He chose four to ride rear guard, another four to fan out up front with him. The rest, he said, should go out ahead and hunt up some meat. He told all of them to keep their eyes open for trouble.

One of the men cleared his throat and raised a hand. "Uh . . . what kind of trouble, mister?"

"Indians. Other white men. Anythin' you don't like the look of, you come fetch me or Matt here."

Within half an hour they were back on the move.

At last the day waned and Sam spurred out ahead to scout up a decent campsite. He found one a mile or so further along the trail and quickly marked out a rough circle some eighty yards in diameter. Not long after that, he was herding the wagons into position so that when the final one was shunted into place, the whole lot together formed a fairly secure circle.

3

SHORTLY after the livestock was secured on a large patch of ground between the wagons and the nearby river, the hunters came in with the selection of game. Sam had heard the distant crack of their long guns all afternoon. Now he saw that they'd downed several grouse, a few antelope and a couple of sage hens. It was hardly enough to feed a hundred and fifty people, of course, but certainly enough to supplement what supplies they'd already brought with them.

Dead on their feet, the pioneers built cook-fires and broke out skillets in preparation for a quick evening meal before sleep. The camp had a curious quietness about it. Even the children were too fatigued to play.

Reverend Berry had invited Sam and Matt to share the evening meal with him and his sister. By the time they turned up at the preacher's wagon, Berry had erected a few crude camp chairs and a fold-away camp table. Here and there within the circle, Sibley tents, half-faced camps and conical bivouacs had been set up, whitened by approaching moonlight, daubed with amber from the many small cook-fires. It was a sharp but bracing evening, and as the folks settled down to eat, someone somewhere produced a guitar upon which to strum the kind of mournful, tear-jerking ballads these sentimental Easterners were so fond of.

The food was simple but nourishing; fried cakes, beans and buffalo steaks swimming in gravy made from hot fat and flour. There was one awkward moment when Sam and Matt went to dig in before the reverend had a chance to say grace, but apart from that, the evening proved to be surprisingly pleasant.

Jessica Berry said not a word,

however, seemingly content to listen to the men. She was a sour-faced woman, about forty, thin of face, hard of eye, but one hell of a good cook.

After the meal, the reverend brought out a clay pipe and Sam lit up a cigar. It had been a hard day but their progress had been good, and now the men were feeling expansive. As Jessica gathered the plates together, Sam said, "That was a real good fare, ma'am. We're mightily obliged."

Jessica merely nodded and broke the habit of a lifetime by smiling.

As she moved away, holding the dishes in a pile before her, Sam remarked to Berry, "She doesn't say much, your sister. Some shy around men, I 'spect."

The sky-pilot shook his head sadly, watching as Sam's fat tan and white cat stalked off to find a comfortable spot beneath his wagon. "The Good Lord did not see fit to bless her with a voice, I am afraid. The poor woman is dumb. But as you say, she is also shy among men, disadvantaged as she is by her affliction."

"Aw, I'm sorry to hear that, reverend, I should've thought — "

"No matter. Perhaps I should have explained."

To save Sam embarrassment, Matt spoke up. "Do you have a veterinarian along with you, reverend? Or someone who knows animals?"

"Our two doctors have served as veterinarians on occasion, Mr Dury. Why?"

"I was just thinkin'. It might be wise to give your livestock a look-over every so often. I don't have to tell you how important the animals are to you, sir. One of 'em gets an infection, they could *all* go down with it."

Berry weighed his comments. "Hmm, that is true. Perhaps I should arrange some kind of regular inspection."

"I'd say that's wise."

"An' one other thing while we're about it," said Sam.

Berry's blue eyes narrowed behind

the wire frames of his spectacles. "Yes, Mr Judge?"

"You hear any talk around Fort Tierney about a feller calls hisself Django Reilly?"

Berry nodded. "Of course. The adjutant back at the fort warned us quite forcibly about the man."

"Well, if he decides to try robbin' this here train, we figure to deal with him pretty much as we did with Galveston Jones an' his buddies. It could get messy if things work out that way, and maybe the men we got ridin' advance guard ought to know it."

The sky-pilot studied his pipe. "I understand what you are saying, Mr Judge. It could be that the men will want no part in a fight, should one come to pass."

Sam chewed his cigar over to the corner of his mouth. "I think you misunderstand me, reverend. I want you to tell the men so's they're *prepared* to fight, not so they can duck out of it." He paused. "Lot of folks got no stomach for fightin', an' I don't condemn a one of 'em. But out here, a man sometimes has to fight whether he wants to or not, if he's to hold onto what he's got. He can't always leave it to the other feller."

Reverend Berry nodded sadly. "I can see the truth of your words," he said quietly. "And while I detest violence, I have learned that one fights fire *with* fire in this harsh land. I will tell them to prepare — and I will also pray that we do not encounter this villain."

"I'm obliged."

At last Sam got to his feet and took up his hat. "Well, it's been a swell evenin', reverend, but I can see you're about as tired as most of these other good folks, so we'll bid you goodnight." He dipped his head to Jessica. "Ma'am."

She nodded back shyly.

"Up at four in the mornin', reverend," Matt reminded him, "an' on the move by seven."

"Very good, Mr Dury. Goodnight to you."

As the Texans strode off through the darkness with Mitzi padding along at their heels, Matt announced his intention to check the perimeter one last time to make sure the pickets they'd posted earlier were still on duty.

"Good idea," Sam replied. "You know what some o' these sissy Easterners're like. They got no stayin'-power."

Sam watched the younger man walk away. Matt's movements were smooth and confident, but there was no swagger to him at all. No man could wish for a better partner, though. Matt had sided him in enough violent donnybrooks to have proved himself time and again.

He sighed. Judge and Dury. That's how it had been back in his old Texas Ranger days, except that the Dury in question then had been Matt's pa, Bob. But even this statement required some amendment, for the truth of the matter was that Bob had not fathered the young man at all. Sam had.

Even now he felt ashamed just to think about it. But though he and Bob were like brothers, Sam was still a man, and Bob's wife had been a mighty fine woman. A moment of loneliness had coupled with a moment of weakness, and before long Rose Dury was heavy with child.

Sam ground his cigar-stub out. Ol' Bob, he'd never doubted that Matt was his boy. Right up to the moment he died, he was just as proud of Matt as any father could be. And Sam sure wasn't about to disillusion him.

Now it was the same with Matt. They were father and son, tied together by blood, but Matt didn't know it and Sam would never tell him. Let him hold the memory of his folks clean and unspoilt. That was the least Sam could do.

"Good evening, Mr Judge."

Sam turned sharply as he surfaced from his reverie and came face to face with Charlotte Minto. The attractive redhead was wrapped in a heavy fur coat as protection against the cool evening air. She still wore that dainty bonnet atop her lustrous, curly hair, though, and as she ran her large brown eyes over him, he caught a whiff of lavender water on her that struck him as mighty alluring.

"He favours you," she remarked, nodding in the direction Matt had taken.

He looked at her closely. What did she mean by that? Had she somehow looked into his mind and read his thoughts? He cleared his throat. "Me'n his pa shared the same colourin'," he explained. Belatedly he touched his fingers to his hat brim. "Help you, Mrs Minto?"

"I was just visiting Mrs Spielmann. She is expecting, you see, quite soon now, I think, and she is understandably anxious. She should have stayed behind at Fort Tierney, really, but such is her determination to reach Spruce Valley that she wouldn't hear of it."

"She's lucky you've got a couple of

sawbones along, if'n you ask me," Sam replied rather ungraciously. "I've led trains across the country where you couldn't find a doctor for love nor money. Watched a lot of sick folks die that way, too."

There wasn't a whole lot Mrs Minto could say to that, so she changed the subject. "It is so nice to stretch one's legs after so many hours aboard one of these wretched wagons, don't you think?"

He shrugged. "I guess." Deciding to take advantage of the situation, he said, "Can I walk you back to your quarters, ma'am?"

Her smile was dazzling. "Why, thank you, Mr Judge." She looked up at his profile as they set off. "May I ask you something?"

"Sure. Can't promise to answer it, o' course."

She smiled politely. "I was just wondering why you changed your mind about guiding us. When we spoke in that stable this afternoon, you did not appear to have a very high opinion of 'Easterners'."

He shrugged. "I jus' got to thinkin', is all. Figured you people could use a little help."

"Oh, come now, Mr Judge. Forgive me for saying so, but you strike me as being a rather uncharitable man. There must have been *some* reason for your coming after us the way you did."

He cracked a rare grin. "The wagon-master's fee."

Her chuckle was throaty and warm. "I am certain Reverend Berry was not *that* generous!"

They came to a narrow break in the wagons and by mutual consent paused a while to look out across the star-washed prairie. The sky was a purple bowl, the flats an endless expanse of rolling grassland. The sharp night air carried cooking smells to them, also a child's occasional laughter and the mournful balladeering of the guitar-player.

"Reverend Berry is right, you know,"

she said after a moment. "Spruce Valley really *will* be the closest thing to Zion on this continent. And shall I tell you why?"

Trying to sound interested, he said, "Sure."

"Because we are all like-minded souls here, Mr Judge," she explained. "*That* is why. We have a common purpose, you see. We want to forge a new way of life for ourselves, a life unsullied by crime and corruption. Ours will be a land where every man, woman and child can depend upon his neighbour, a land where guns will be used only to put meat on the table, where there are things more important than money. We have doctors with us, as you know, teachers, farmers, men of trade, and women to bear them fine, healthy children. We will raise crops, Mr Judge. I am told the soil is good for everything from buckwheat to peaches. Cattle will proliferate in the valley. We *will* enjoy paradise here on earth."

"I sure hope so, ma'am. You

people're pinnin' just about ever'thin' you got on the notion."

They continued walking. At last the Minto wagon came into sight. Charlotte paused again then, and turned to look up at the tall, lean man beside her. "Shall I tell you something, Mr Judge?" she asked quietly.

"If you feel you ought to."

"I *know* why you decided to come after us."

That little pronouncement gave him a start. She *knew* that he and Matt were hoping the wagon train would draw Django Reilly out into the open? Maybe she *could* read minds after all. "You, ah . . . you do?" he prompted at last.

"Yes," she replied. "And I am very flattered, sir. And though it may be considered bold of me to say it, say it I will; should you wish to call upon me at any time during the remainder of this journey, Mr Judge . . . Samuel . . . you would be *most* welcome."

He looked down at her, his own

face hidden by the shadow thrown by his hat-brim. Well, if that didn't beat all! The woman actually thought he'd changed his mind because of her! Well . . . she *had* been a consideration, of course, but only one of several, and he found it a little off-putting to hear her now, convinced as she was that she alone was responsible for his being here. Curiously, it made him think of Jessica Berry, of her appealing shyness and modesty, and that confused him even more.

"Uh . . . well, I thank you for the invite, ma'am, I surely do," he said, slowly backing away from her. "Maybe I'll take you up on it sometime."

"I look forward to it, sir."

He touched the brim of his hat in farewell, turned and got the hell out of there, feeling vaguely threatened by her boldness and just a little dwarfed by the enormity of her ego.

★ ★ ★

The wagon train rolled westward across the grassy flats. The plains stretched away on all sides, bordered by far mountains, thick strands of timber and the rushing, winding river. Blue stem grew thick and tall hereabouts, its natural green colour tinged with the faintest touch of turquoise. Further west, where the rainfall was appreciably less, the blue stem would eventually give way to shorter wire grass, the wire grass to more tufted buffalo grass. Pretty soon after that the land would begin to shelve up towards the distant, timbered mountains, and Spruce Valley.

Out ahead of the column, Sam rode his gnarled old roan through the stirrup-high grass, his mild grey eyes searching for any sign of trouble. In the distance he heard the occasional crack of rifle-fire and knew that the hunters were keeping busy. Reining in, he hipped around to watch the canvas-topped column rattling slowly on. The wagons stretched back as far as the eye could see.

Absently he reached behind him. His questing fingers finally found his cat's furry head projecting from the saddlebag and he began to rub between the animal's pointed ears. Mitzi gave a low purr of contentment.

Back down the line, teams of oxen or draft-horses hauled their burdens doggedly on beneath the gradually strengthening Nebraska sun. Here a young woman cradled a restless baby and made silly nonsense sounds to stop its crying. There a big-bellied Swedish farmer walking beside his team had to rest a moment to ease his aching feet. Mrs Spielmann lay in back of her cluttered wagon, hands clasped across her swollen stomach. Her baby would come soon, now. She could feel it. She had been through this twice before. She knew all the portents. But still she felt anxious.

The column moved on amid the sounds of rattling chains, squeaking axles, turning wheels and plodding hooves. Matt kept his cow-pony moving back and forth along the line, keeping them tight and orderly, making sure he always caught Rachel Minto's pale blue eyes as he passed her wagon, and never missed an opportunity to tip his hat to the girl or exchange some small pleasantry or word of encouragement.

Still, it was a boring, mind-numbing routine from which there was little relief. These people had already put many hundreds of miles behind them. There was no longer any wonder left in them for this enormous, wide-open land. About an hour after the noon break, however, Matt was alerted by a high, wooden crack and a woman's scream, and turned his horse quickly to go track it down.

About three-quarters of the way down the line, one of the wagons had come to a halt, holding up everyone behind it. As Matt rode closer, he saw why. A few spokes on the left-side rear wheel had shattered and the weight of the wagon had snapped and buckled the iron tyre.

Now the Conestoga was listing slightly to one side, like a ship floundering at sea.

As Matt reined in, the owner of the wagon, a skinny, forty-some man with a black beard sketching his weak jaw like a horseshoe, looked up at him. "I . . . I've run into a little trouble here. Will you lend me a hand, brother? I have a spare wheel beneath the wagon, but I won't be able to fix it on my own."

Matt glanced up at the man's wife, who was sitting on the wagon's high seat surrounded by several young children, all of whom looked pretty shaken up by the accident. "All right. Just let me get these other folks movin'. We'll catch up with 'em later."

"Thank you, friend."

Matt kneed his pony down to the next wagon in line and raised his voice. "All right, folks. You'll have to back up an' go around."

The thick-lipped man standing beside his wall-eyed oxen frowned. "*Was?*" he asked in puzzlement.

"You'll have to back up an' go around."

The man shook his head. He had no American. Matt swallowed a curse. He repeated his instructions a third time, adding a few quick gestures to make the German comprehend his meaning. At last the man nodded and smiled genially. "Ah, *ja, ja. Ich begriefen.*"

The big Prussian worked his wagon around the stalled Conestoga and the wagons lined up behind him followed his example while Matt backed his pony off to the side of the trail and watched them go. The little man with the horseshoe beard introduced himself as Cyrus Kennedy from Harrisburg, Pennsylvania, then set about helping his wife and children down from the listing wagon.

A short time later, a big man in a Murphy wagon near the end of the line hailed them when he was near enough and asked if they needed any help.

Matt could tell from the rattling

contents of the man's vehicle that he was a blacksmith by trade, and nodded. "Sure. Thanks."

The man stalled his wagon and jumped down. He gave his name as Sparks Wilson from New York State, then took one look at the damaged wheel and said, "We'll have to jack the wagon back up and hold it there with some flat rocks so we can change the wheel without havin' to rush it. Let's take a look around and see what we can find for leverage."

They set to work as the last of the wagons trundled slowly past them and disappeared into the pall of dust ahead.

It took some time, but eventually the three men were able to fashion some kind of crude lever system from a stout log pole and a pile of rocks, and hoist the wagon high enough to effect a repair while Kennedy's wife and children watched them from the side of the military road. Even so, it was hard toil, though Sparks Wilson seemed to know what he was about, and worked with dexterous efficiency to finish the job in half the time it would have taken Matt and Kennedy alone.

They were just finishing up when Matt started to get the feeling that they were being watched. He realised also in that moment that the rest of the wagon train had disappeared from sight and that they were all alone on the breezy prairie.

He straightened up, leaving his two male companions to tighten the hub of the new wheel to the axle assembly and top it off with a lick of grease, his nape itching stronger now. Keeping his hands down at his sides and close to the grips of his Tranters, he turned around slowly to face their backtrail.

Seven weapon-heavy Indians, Cheyenne, he thought, sat their painted horses about twenty yards away, fanned out across the trail. One of them, older than the rest, his bronzed body just turning from muscle to fat, was distinguishable from the others by an enormous feathered war bonnet complete with trailers. Apart from that, each man there wore a trade breechclout, metal arm bands, buckskin shirts and leggings trimmed with fancy beadwork. They appeared regal, with large, hooked noses, high, pronounced cheekbones and square jaws. They wore their black hair with a centre parting and two braids. The oldest man there, the fellow wearing the war bonnet, was in his late forties, the youngest perhaps nineteen. Their horses were painted with lightning streaks and coloured balls. Most of them also sported handprints, to show that their owners had killed at least one enemy in battle. Certainly the Cheyennes themselves were loaded for bear, with an assortment of cut-down long guns, lances, clubs, bows and knives.

Matt had been expecting to see them, or something very much like them, but even though he was almost prepared for it, the sight of them still made the breath catch in his throat. He locked into position, facing them, telling himself to show no fear and no surprise, and above all, give them no reason to use the weapons they were brandishing so readily.

★ ★ ★

The afternoon wore on. Progress was slow but steady. The hunters continued to puncture the air with occasional bursts of gunfire. Eventually Sam fell back a little to ride alongside Reverend Berry's wagon.

The preacher's round face was sweat-run and florid. The hardships of the trail were obviously taking their toll on him, although he managed a pleasant enough greeting when Sam rode up.

"Ah, good . . . good afternoon, Mr Judge. Is everything in . . . in order?"

"Uh-huh," Sam replied. "We'll give it about another hour, then see what we can do about settin' up night-camp."

"Very good." The reverend indicated

78

some debris beside the trail, now overgrown with grass and wildflowers, and warped by the elements. "It is sad, don't you think? A chair here, a chest there. Remnants of those souls who passed this way in the earliest days of expansion."

Sam, who had been seeing discarded items of furniture off and on all day, nodded and turned his attention to Jessica, who was seated patiently up on the wagon. Ma'am, I wonder if I might ask you a favour?"

The woman appeared surprised by the question, but recovered quickly and spread her hands in a gesture he took to mean *go ahead*.

"It's my cat, Mitzi," he explained, reaching behind him to scoop the lardy feline from his saddlebag. "I figure she's gettin' awful cramped, ridin' up here with me. Could be she'll feel more at home up there in the box with you. Will you look after her for me?"

Jessica's dark eyes moved from the cat to Sam's face. She nodded. He heeled his horse a bit closer and passed the cat across to her. "I'm obliged, ma'am."

As she took the cat, her cheeks flushed with the slightest hint of pink.

Sam twisted around in the saddle, so that he could look back down the line, and frowned. Reverend Berry saw the expression and asked, "Is there something the matter, Mr Judge?"

Sam shrugged. "Have you seen Matt just lately, reverend?"

"Not recently," the preacher replied, glancing over one shoulder. Normally, the younger man could nearly always be seen tooling his horse up and down the line, keeping them all moving, but now there was no sign of him.

"Think maybe I'll go find him," Sam muttered half to himself.

He backed the gnarled old strawberry roan around and sent it back along the line, drawing down only when he came to Charlotte Minto's wagon.

The handsome redhead was dressed in a plainer and prettier checked cotton dress today and a thick, sensible jacket similar to that worn by her daughter Rachel, who was riding a high-stepping young pony on the far side of the wagon. When Sam came up to them, he turned Charlie back to the southwest so that he could ride alongside.

"Afternoon, ma'am. Miss Rachel."

Charlotte was all smiles. "Why, Mr Judge. How nice of you to come calling."

"I was just wondering if you've seen anything of Matt around here lately."

Charlotte thought for a moment. "No. No, I haven't seen him for some time. Rachel?"

Physically, Rachel was a younger version of her mother, although her features had a somewhat softer look to them, and her blue eyes had about them an appealing innocence. Neither was she the same kind of fashion-plate as her mother, preferring boys'-size pants and hardwearing shirts, at least while she was on the trail.

She shook her head. "I saw him

81

about an hour ago. No, more than an hour." Her expression grew concerned. "Is there anything wrong, do you think, Mr Judge?"

Sam inclined his shoulders. "I doubt it. Just wondered where he'd got to, that's all. Maybe he's helpin' someone down at the tail-end of the train. I'll go see."

"Do you mind if I ride along with you?" the young girl asked. She rubbed a palm along the pony's glistening neck. "Bonnie could use some exercise."

Sam glanced up at Charlotte. "That be all right, ma'am?"

Charlotte nodded. "Just don't be too long, Rachel."

Back down the trail, Matt had stayed exactly where he was, not daring to take his eyes off the Cheyennes sitting their horses twenty yards distant. He heard Kennedy's wife make the softest sound, as if she were stifling her scream instead of letting it rip, and knew without turning around that she had seen them, too.

That alerted Kennedy and Sparks. Matt heard Kennedy say, "*What* — ?", then go quiet.

Still the Cheyennes sat their ponies, watching them from out of expressionless red faces.

Sparks came up straight, a bear of a man with a flushed, good-natured face now turned flinty. Very slowly he came over to stand beside Matt, the two of them forming a barrier that would provide no protection at all for the woman and the children if the Indians decided to make trouble.

"Mr Dury," the blacksmith said from the corner of his mouth. "I got a Manhattan pistol right here in my back pocket, if you want to make a fight of it."

Matt had already considered making a fight of it. But there were the unfavourable odds to consider, the presence of the woman and children, the fact that, up until Sparks had told him about the Manhattan pistol, he'd believed himself to be the only armed white man among them. And then again, the Indians had given him no reason — so far — to suggest that they actually *were* looking for trouble.

So he shook his head at Sparks' suggestion and whispered back, "I wouldn't advise it. Try mixin' it up with these fellers and I'll lay generous odds we'd arrive in the Happy Hunting Ground long before they do."

Still, one thing was certain; they couldn't just stand around here the entire day, just staring at each other. Like it or not, someone was going to have to break the ice. So, moving real slow, Matt raised his right hand and held it palm up. The Indians watched him inscrutably.

"Any of you fellers speak English?" he asked, not holding out too much hope.

The Indians continued to stare at him, making no move to speak, no move to return the hand signal for peace.

They stayed like that for maybe half

a minute more, until into the tableau came the sound of horses' hooves. Instinct told Matt that Sam must've come out to find them, and though he knew they were by no means out of the woods yet, he felt a surge of relief. Suddenly the odds looked a little better, should it come to fighting.

He didn't dare take his eyes off the Cheyennes until he saw that they had stopped watching him in order to view the approach of the newcomers. Then he too chanced a look over his shoulder just as Sam and a second rider — dammit, that was Rachel Minto up there! — reined in a dozen yards away.

Matt frowned. What the hell was Rachel doing here? The question began to form on his lips, but before he could voice it, Sam shut him up with a sharp shake of the head.

Silence thickened and bore down on the assembly as the man from Texas ran his mild grey eyes across the redmen. Their lazy-stitch beadwork alone was enough to identify them as Cheyenne, never mind the long, lean, sky-blue arrows in their quivers and steel-studded clubs hanging from bands around their wrists. Question was; were these Northern, or Southern, Cheyennes? The difference was crucial. Those Indians from the south tended to be more of a passive disposition, while their northern brothers were frequently out-and-out mean.

He ran his eyes over each face there. The atmosphere was charged with tension. He knew in his heart then that these Indians were Northern Cheyennes; and worse, that they were Dog Soldiers, quite probably the deadliest cavalry in the whole wide world.

4

THE Indians were returning his appraisal. He wondered where they had come from and what they were doing here. A few years earlier, Dull Knife, Little Wolf and a few hundred others had jumped their reservation down in Indian Territory and come north, figuring to head for Montana. They'd made it as far as northeastern Nebraska, then the army had caught up with 'em and locked 'em away at Fort Robinson. There'd been an escape attempt not so long after that, and the army had shot or otherwise slaughtered fifty of them. Maybe these fellers were part of a band that had gotten away.

Sam kneed Charlie a little closer, the better to converse with them. You could not afford to show these warriors your fear. You had to try and take command of the situation and impress them with your courage.

All eyes were on him as he looped his reins around his saddlehorn and began to move his hands in a series of quick gestures. First, he held his right palm up to them, then pointed and brought his left hand across his chest, flat. Next, he brought his right hand down to rub the left twice, from wrist to knuckles, before using both index fingers to make a slashing motion.

The Indians showed surprise. Clearly they had not been expecting him to address them in *Wibluto*, the sign language of the plains. Meanwhile, Sam continued to let his hands do the talking. Keeping his right hand flat and chest-high, he moved it in a horizontal circle from his left to right. He raised his right hand in front of his neck, palm out, index and second finger extended skyward, then brought the tips of his fingers up as far as the brim of his Stetson.

The Indian wearing the war bonnet

urged his horse forward at a walk, halting it with knee pressure alone when no more than two or three feet separated their horses' heads. Charlie, smelling the wild aggression of the Cheyenne pony, sidestepped a little, while Sam slowly reached into the pocket of his buttoned-to-the-throat grey jacket and fetched out two cigars. He passed one to the chief, bit the end off his own, stuck it in his mouth and searched for some matches.

Once they had their smokes lit, Sam started up again. The Cheyennes watched intently. Sam held his flattened right hand in front of his body, moved it back to the right, pointed forward and down. Then he raised his fingers out front and upwards. He pushed both hands up, then held up the left and struck it twice with the right, and repeated the gesture all over again. More gestures followed, including a symbolic clasping of hands.

After a while he finished whatever it was he'd been saying. Now it was the Indian's turn. The gestures meant little to Matt. Sam watched him for a moment, then gestured that the Indian should take it a little slower, and nodded when the pace was right. He sat quietly, 'listening', then pointed at the chief with his left hand and added some other signs.

Whatever Sam had said made the Cheyenne chief ponder for a moment. At last he raised his right hand and pointed up at the sky with his forefinger, then let the hand drop. By way of reply, Sam held his right hand out to the side, formed an incomplete circle with his thumb and forefinger and slowly let the hand drop about twelve inches.

The Cheyenne nodded his understanding and backed his horse away. He turned the animal so that he was facing his companions again and let out a stream of ugly, guttural speech. The other Indians listened for a moment. One of them appeared to argue with him. The chief had the last word, though, and like it or not, his word was law. A moment later they swung their painted ponies around and kicked them into a gallop south and east, across the prairie.

Matt and the others watched them go. Kennedy and his wife were hugging their children close. Rachel was sitting her fine pony up beside Sparks' wagon. Into the silence came some low muttering, and when Matt glanced around, it was to see the blacksmith from New York mopping his sweaty face and saying some kind of prayer.

Up on the roan, Sam allowed his shoulders to drop a little as he sighed.

"What the heck was that all about?" Matt asked at last.

Sam looked around. The recently-repaired wagon told its own story and confirmed what he'd already suspected. "The chief calls hisself Shield-That-Shatters. They're Northern Cheyenne, part of a bunch that live an' hunt southeast of here."

"What did they want with us?" Sparks asked.

"The same thing Indians always want."

"Sc-scalps?" Cyrus Kennedy asked with a gulp.

Sam said, "Food. Tobacco. Trade goods — blankets, knives and the like. They say they've been watchin' us for the past couple of days. Readin' betwixt the lines, I think they decided against showin' themselves in case some of you greenhorns started shootin' at 'em, but when they saw you fellers out here all by yourselves, they figured to come in and try to scare you out of a few supplies."

"So they're nothing but a band of cowards!" Sparks said in disgust.

Sam's face turned hard. "They're anything *but* cowards, mister. But they'd as soon not get involved in any fightin' trouble, an' I can't say as I blame 'em. They've been hounded for ten, twenty years now. There's hardly any of 'em left. While these fellers here can still live their lives like half-way free men, they'll try not to do anything that'll bring the army down on 'em again. But you push 'em and they'll fight like tigers, and if you don't believe me, just try it."

It went quiet for a moment, until Kennedy rediscovered some of the courage that had deserted him a few minutes earlier. "I hope you told them that we white men don't give in to the demands of such heathens, brother."

"I went one better than that," Sam replied easily. "I told 'em to come callin' at around seven o'clock tonight, 'cause we'd be plumb proud to make 'em some kind'a peace offerin' in return for safe passage."

Cyrus Kennedy and Sparks Wilson both looked scandalised by the suggestion. In unison they said, "You did *what*?"

★ ★ ★

Forty minutes later, Reverend Berry said the self-same thing. "You did *what*, Mr Judge?"

93

Sam took a fresh cigar from his pocket and lit up. He wasn't used to having to explain his actions to others. If these people trusted him to get them where they were headed in one piece, they ought to trust his judgement in other matters, too. But perhaps it was as well that they understand *why* they were going to do as he said.

He looked around. Once they'd reached the head of the column again, Matt and Rachel had gone on ahead to mark out a campsite. Now the wagons were rolling past the reverend's stalled prairie schooner in a slow, dusty procession, with the would-be settlers giving him some mighty curious stares.

"The way I see it, you got two choices, reverend," he replied at length. "You either *give* the Indians what they want, or they'll *take* it. And I can promise you, givin' will be a whole lot less painful than havin' the Cheyennes takin' whatever they want."

Berry blanched. "You mean they will

turn aggressive?" he asked.

"That's exactly what I mean. So we invite 'em in, make a performance out of greetin' them and givin' 'em whatever we can spare, and maybe — maybe — they'll be satisfied with that and leave us to make the rest of our journey in peace."

"Can we not try to out-distance them?" the sky-pilot asked. "You told them to come at sunset. It's only four o'clock now. That gives us at least three clear hours — "

"I never yet saw the wagon that could outdistance an Indian pony," Sam replied. "Besides which, I've given them my word. Man breaks his word to the Indians, it could go bad for all the whites who come after him."

He blew foul-smelling grey smoke into the afternoon air. "Pass the word, reverend," he said, taking up the roan's trailing reins. "I want your people to treat these Indians with respect when they come ridin' in tonight. I want the women to cook up all kinds o' sweetmeats they can take away with 'em and the men to cough up whatever they can spare in the way of gee-gaws, blankets and the like. I'll expect everyone to donate a little something to the pile, and it had better be good, cause I'll be usin' it to buy our safe passage. Tell you what. Get Mrs Minto to organise that — she can be a mighty persuasive talker when she gets goin'."

As he swung aboard the gnarled horse, he flashed a smile at Jessica Berry, who was sitting up on the stalled schooner with Mitzi in her arms, and tipped his hat to her. This time she met his gaze without looking away, and returned his smile with one of her own.

Camp was set up in half the time it usually took, and as word spread about the identity of their visitors, so the flat, grass-rich site became a hive of nervous activity. As the sun began its westward slide, so the cool evening air grew redolent with the spicy smells of baking and frying. Torches were lit to throw an uncertain amber glow down over the proceedings. Men clustered together to discuss the imminent arrival of the savages. Some suggested they use the opportunity to prepare an ambush and simply shoot them down when they rode in. That didn't sound much like the kind of charity Sam had expected to hear from good people headed for the nearest thing to almighty Zion on the face of the continent, and he put an end to it pretty quick. The whole point of going to all this fuss in the first place was to *avoid* trouble, after all. And if the settlers *did* start anything, they could be damn' certain the Cheyennes would finish it.

"But Sparks Wilson said they wuz only seven of them, Judge," said a man named Comaskey. "Seven Injuns agin *seventy* white men!"

"There was only seven that we could *see*," Sam replied. "That's the difference, mister. A difference it'd pay you fellers to bear in mind."

Comaskey wasn't convinced, though.

"I still don't see why we should have to kow-tow to these heathens."

"Then let me put it another way," Sam told him, fixing him with a cold, hard stare. "The safety of every man, woman an' child on this train depends on how we treat these Cheyennes. So make no mistake about it; I'll kill the first man here who tries to make trouble with 'em when they arrive. You got that? I won't ask for no excuses an' I won't be givin' any second chances. I'll just shoot him where he stands an' have him buried where he falls."

At last approaching sunset began to draw gold and scarlet streamers across the dusky sky. Slowly all the preparations reached their various conclusions. An impressive mountain of trade goods grew at the centre of the camp. The only thing left now was simply to await the arrival of the Cheyennes.

Matt was down near the river, seeing to his pony at the rope corral on the north side of the camp when he caught the soft sound of approaching foot steps and turned quickly, his nerves stretched taut just like those of all the settlers. He allowed himself to relax a touch when he recognised Rachel Minto coming towards him from out of the darkness.

"I'm sorry," she said when she was close enough to talk without having to break the uneasy silence with a shout. "I didn't mean to startle you."

He greeted her with a broad smile, admiring the pale alabaster of her complexion, the youthful wonder in her large eyes, the childlike tilt of her nose contrasted with the womanly swell of her full lips. She had changed from her tomboyish trail-wear, he saw, and looked stunning in a powder-blue dress trimmed with white lace that moulded the curves and swells of her body.

"I guess we're all a little jumpy right now," he allowed. "Anyway, what're you doing out here all by yourself? I don't think it's a very good idea to stray too far from your wagon at the moment. 'Fact, if you've got any sense, you'll try to stay out of sight."

"What, and miss the chance of seeing some of those Indians up close?"

He took her arm and began to lead her back toward the wagons. "Weren't they close enough this afternoon?" he asked.

She glanced up at him shyly. "About this afternoon, Matt. That's really why I came to find you. I wanted to tell you . . . "

"Hm?"

"I thought it was incredibly brave of you, the way you faced up to those Cheyennes. You would have taken them all on, wouldn't you? If you'd thought they were going to attack Mrs Kennedy and the others?"

He shrugged. "I'd have given it a good try," he replied honestly. "But I was awful glad that Sam showed up when he did."

"He means a lot to you, doesn't he? Your Uncle Sam?"

Matt didn't even have to consider his

response. "I got in with a bad crowd just after my ma died and I quit Texas," he explained awkwardly. "No, that's not right. They weren't really bad, just . . . just young, I guess. Well, them other fellers, they did a terrible thing. They robbed a bank and killed some people, one of 'em just a kid, and when Sam caught up with 'em, the law hung 'em." He stopped and turned to face her. "They could've hung me, too, if it hadn't been for Sam showin' me the error o' my ways." He shrugged again and gave a self-conscious little laugh to try and lighten the moment. "I don't suppose there's any real way to say just how you feel about a man who's given you back not only your life but some of your self-respect, too."

"I like your Uncle Sam," Rachel remarked as they continued walking. "I don't think he's as irascible as he likes to pretend. My mother likes him, too."

Matt laughed with more humour this time. "Well, let me tell you, he sure likes — "

Rachel stiffened suddenly. "What is it, Matt?"

Matt's face had been wiped of all its humour. Now, in the weak, flickering glow of the burning faggots, it looked hard and stony, older than its twenty three years. "They're comin'," he replied in a low, urgent tone, and she heard it too, then; the steady, distant drum of approaching horses. "Come on, let's get you safely under canvas before they get here."

Sam had given instructions earlier in the afternoon that the wagons were to be set up in the shape of a giant horseshoe, with the break facing the east. For one thing, it would make it easier for the Indians to enter and leave camp. For another, it would make them feel at home, for that was how they always chose to erect their own *tipis*.

Now, standing at the centre of the camp, hearing the steadily increasing thunder of unshod horse-hooves, he felt his guts tense. He knew that, deep down, these Cheyennes wanted to avoid a fight like the plague. Any serious confrontation between white man and red would bring the army out to these remote flats to hunt them to extinction. But that was the trouble with Indians; you could never be *sure*. About the only thing predictable about them, in fact, was their very unpredictability.

Reverend Berry was standing beside him. Now the preacher uttered his name. Sam glanced down at him and said, "Yeah?"

The preacher looked ghastly. "I think I'm going to be sick," he said, grimacing.

"Stick with it, reverend. It's only nerves. Say a prayer or somethin'."

"I don't believe I've stopped praying since this entire business started," Berry replied.

"Well, just try not to spew up all over the guests until I've had my say, all right?"

He saw them then, coming out of the night-shadows of the prairie and into the amber arena formed by the covered wagons, and he drew in a startled breath because the seven Cheyennes he'd parlayed with earlier had somehow turned into twenty five or thirty.

They came in at a gallop, muscular ponies painted in reds and yellows, the men themselves — he'd known they would leave their squaws and papooses back in their own distant encampment — painted in all kinds of styles and resplendent in their beaded buckskins.

They came to a halt before Sam and the reverend and Mrs Minto and one or two others who had somehow come to find themselves saddled with the responsibility of forming a welcoming committee, fanned out, sat their wall-eyed horses in a line, faintly blurred around the edges by slowly-settling dust.

Sam met their stares and did not back away. He recognised Shield-That-Shatters at the approximate centre of the group, and nodded a slow, cautious greeting. The Dog Soldier chief had painted one side of his face yellow, the other side red. There was no sound now, nothing at all save the odd bawling of a disturbed and half-asleep baby, the occasional snort of a blowing, shifting horse.

For their part, the Indians glanced around, studying the emigrants standing beside their wagons looking right back at them, with the kind of haughty disdain they might ordinarily reserve for their comrades, the Sioux. The tension in the air was undeniable. Sam remembered the warning he'd passed around to the settlers. God help the man who chose to get trigger-happy. But then again, if it came to fighting, God help them *all*.

At last Sam took a pace forward and raised his hands to 'speak', but the brave astride the pony to the left of Shield-That-Shatters urged the animal forward.

"There is no need for *Wibluto*," he said in a low, gravelly tone. "I speak your tongue." He had a long,

105

copper face framed by shoulder-length, raven-black hair. His eyes were two smouldering coals, his nose an ugly beak, his lips thick, without humour. He was perhaps the same age as Matt. "I am the son of Shield-That-Shatters," he said. "Red Blade."

Sam nodded as Matt, having escorted Rachel back to her wagon, came over to join them. The man from Texas said, "Howdy, Red Blade. Why don't you an' your buddies light an' set a spell? We got some gifts here for you that ought to make your squaws real happy."

He indicated the gathered blankets and bolts of cloth, patchwork quilts and old skillets, but saw nothing in the Indians' faces to suggest approval or otherwise. He thought he read something in their glittering eyes, though, as they surveyed the bullet moulds and hardtack and dried fruit and flannel shirts and goggles, sunbonnets, campstools, shovels, whetstones, airtights and chamberpots. They could use these things, he knew; even the small and seemingly pointless things could improve their status among their own people.

"Light an' set a spell," he said again. "We got tobacco for you and coffee, too, an' some doughnuts that'll just plumb melt in your mouths."

"And firewater?" Red Blade asked.

Sam shook his head. "No."

"You lie."

Sam forced himself to let the insult pass. "These folks're regular church-goers, Red Blade. For them, drinkin' spirits is like a crime the Sky Father would have to punish, was they to do it."

"You lie," Red Blade said again.

The muscles in Sam's face tightened imperceptibly. "I'm tellin' it straight, Red Blade. This here train's dry as a bone. And I'd as soon you didn't call me a liar again."

The young Cheyenne looked around, his glittering eyes finally coming to rest on Charlotte Minto, who squirmed uncomfortably. "You *do* have women," he remarked around a smirk.

Sam nodded. "But not for you."

Red Blade turned to address his father. Not for the first time, Sam wondered why a man speaking Cheyenne always sounded like he was about to puke up. Reverend Berry would probably have spoken the language real good, the way he was feeling right then. At last the Indians climbed down and came ahead to inspect the gifts, surprisingly tall, and walking bow-legged like all horsemen. Some of the tension went out of the situation once they had dismounted. The settlers watched them as they came over, bent to examine the airtights and shovels, to pick up the odd penny whistle or harmonica and warily give it an experimental toot that drew grins and chuckles from their comrades.

Red Blade and Shield-That-Shatters came directly across to Sam. Sam pulled out the last of his cigars and handed them one apiece. As he struck a match and held it to the tip of each brave's smoke, Red Blade said, "My father says, that it is good that you fear Cheyennes, white man."

Sam steeled himself for what he was about to say, because though he didn't want it to sound like fighting talk, the Cheyennes might take it that way. "Well, mayhaps we should put him right about something, Red Blade. We *don't* fear you. There isn't a man, woman or child here who *does*. But we sure as hell respect you."

Red Blade stared right into his face. Sam stared back, unmoved. "We do not have to take these trinkets as gifts, white man," the Cheyenne muttered contemptuously. "We could just as easily take them as spoils of war."

Sam shrugged, trying his best to look mightily unconcerned. "You *could*," he allowed. "But sometimes it takes more strength to set old differences aside and become friends, wouldn't you say? And in any case, where's the point of fightin'? What's to be gained by turnin' our women into widows and our children into orphans? Life is hard for the Plains Indians. It would be harder still for the squaws and little ones whose fathers died for no good reason here tonight, just as it would for the whites."

Red Blade considered this, then translated while Shield-That-Shatters listened without once taking his eyes from Sam's face. At last he did some more jabbering and Red Blade said, "My father says you have much wisdom, for a white man, and he agrees. There are times when a man can prove his strength by *not* fighting."

"I had a feelin' he might see it that way," Sam replied, letting some of the tension ebb out of him. "Now come on, Red Blade, let's go dig into them doughnuts afore the rest of your buddies bolt the lot!"

★ ★ ★

The Cheyennes dug in, all right. Doughnuts, deep-dish, dried-apple pie, black, heavily sweetened coffee — they downed the lot, and soon they were splitting the cool night air with the penny whistles and harmonicas and an old accordion someone had decided to donate to the pile, while some of the braver settlers tried to teach them how to dance white-man fashion. 'Course, the accordion didn't sound so hot after one of the Indians stuck his tomahawk through its folds, but no-one really seemed to mind about that.

Sam, the reverend and Mrs Minto stayed outside of the proceedings, willing the hours to pass without event until the Cheyennes decided that enough was enough, gathered together their 'gifts' and left. And, as luck would have it, things did go peacefully, albeit a tad rambunctious. Only once did an over-exuberant Indian grab hold of one of the emigrant women, but even then Red Blade stepped in to break them up before the girl's father could arrive and start a fight.

Even Red Blade was not to be

trusted completely, though, and on more than one occasion he came across to Sam to ask, "You are *sure* you have no firewater, white man?"

Sam nodded. "I'm sure," he'd reply, though in truth he wasn't sure at all. Still, he could hardly imagine that a pair of zealots like Reverend Berry and Charlotte Minto would allow the settlers to bring a little of the devil's brew into paradise with them.

At last Shield-That-Shatters, looking just a little uncomfortable from all the food he'd put away throughout the course of the evening, passed the word that they were leaving, and reluctantly his braves came back over to their horses and gathered up all the paraphernalia with which Sam had bought their safe passage. They swung aboard their mounts and without bothering to make any kind of farewells to their hosts, simply turned to the east and lit off back onto the moon-whitened plains, rending the air with their yapping cries and leaving only a cloud of twisting dust behind to mark their exit.

The camp was quiet for a time after that, as the settlers slowly let their pent-up tension out. Sam himself sagged up against the wheel of the nearest wagon while, around him, the settlers set about clearing up and gathering together to talk about their encounter with the dreaded neanderthals.

Reverend Berry, having finally overcome his nausea, trotted across to clap him on the arm and shake him by the hand. Adrenalin had left the preacher all fired-up with nervous energy. He felt he could do just about anything tonight. "Mr Judge, the way you handled those Cheyennes was *magnificent*, sir! I don't imagine I shall ever see anything quite so inspiring ever again!"

Sam shrugged. "It was nothin'."

"Ah! Such modesty, too!"

Sam left them all to it, went through a gap between one wagon and the next and strode off to stand a while in the darkness, looking away to the north and west and thinking about the miles they still had to cover.

Some moments later he turned when he heard the tall grass shushing behind him and saw Mitzi slinking towards him with a meow of greeting coming from her mouth. He bent, scooped the cat up, held her at arms'-length and inspected her. The fat Abyssinian looked back at him from out of liquid, sea green eyes and meowed again.

He ruffled the fur between her ears, set her down again, and was just straightening back up when he realised that Jessica Berry, pale-faced, hard-eyed Jessica, with her thin, breastless body hidden beneath an unflattering grey-wool dress and a pale lemon shawl, had followed the cat out into the secluded darkness.

He saw the pale flash of her teeth through the gloom and returned the smile, thinking that just that gesture alone softened her considerably, and made her shed years. "Evenin', ma'am," he said. "Been quite a night, hasn't it?"

She nodded and he wondered how in hell he was going to hold a conversation with a woman who couldn't speak. But somehow that didn't seem to be a problem. He felt comfortable with her, that was the main thing, and he realised that there was no good reason why he should feel any other way.

"We should cross this here river tomorrow, all bein' well," he said as they stood side by side, staring out into the shadows. "An' once we're across the river, we head thataway, northwest. After that, it's a more or less straight run until we hit the mountains."

Again she nodded. He turned and looked at her. She smiled at him some more, a tender, uncertain, genuine smile. The moonlight gentled her otherwise harsh features considerably. She shivered, for the night had turned quite sharp, and pulled her shawl closer around her shoulders, and he knew in that moment, as he looked down into her dark eyes, why she had come out here to find him.

He reached out, took hold of her, drew her to him and kissed her softly on the lips.

There was a moment then when he wondered if he'd read the signs wrong, whether she was going to struggle out of his grip and slap him, but no, he felt the stiffness go out of her, felt her body beneath the plain grey dress melt, and pretty soon after that her arms snaked up across his back to hold him tight and they kissed again.

She hadn't had much experience in kissing, and she was awkward about it. But that didn't matter. In her way, she was beautiful, and her lack of experience was appealing. She was serene, and there was something about her that calmed *him*, too.

He heard the faintest of sounds then, a kind of sharp hiss, and broke the embrace to twist around and face it. He saw a figure standing there in the gap between the two wagons, the face a mixture of surprise and indignation. The figure sucked in some more breath, said something that sounded very much like, "*Oh!*"

"Mrs Minto?" he said, frowning.

She took a step out from between the wagons and moonlight shone faintly off her high-piled red hair. "*Really!*" she hissed. "Mr Judge! And Miss Berry! How *could* you?"

"Ma'am?"

She came closer, which was a good thing, for had she stayed over there by the wagons she would have had to raise her voice to be heard, and that would have alerted the whole camp. "I . . . I thought we had an understanding!" she said, indignant as all get-out.

He frowned some more. "An understandin', ma'am? I don't think so."

She came right out and slapped him across the face then, her rage spilling over. "Then you have a very short memory, sir!" she said. A whole variety of emotions played across her face as she glared up at him. "To think . . . to think that I should find you in the arms of this . . . *this* woman!" Her eyes burned into his face. "What . . . what has this woman got that I have not? Why, she can't even *speak*, for Heaven's sake!"

Sam reached out and grabbed hold of her still-raised hand. "Now you hold it right there," he said sharply, losing his own temper now. "In the first place, the only 'understanding' we had was the one in your imagination, Mrs Minto. In the second place, it's none of your damned beeswax one way or the other what Miss Berry here or me choose to get up to. And in the third place, don't you ever let me hear you bad-mouth this here woman again, 'cause whether she can speak or not, she's still twice the woman you'll *ever* be!"

"Doh!"

The handsome redhead tore herself out of his grip, turned and hurried off amidst a rustling of petticoats.

Sam watched her go, letting the air

out through his long straight nose. *Women!* He'd never understand them!

When he'd calmed down a tad, he turned back to face Jessica Berry. He saw tears glistening on her cheeks, and they served only to make him feel more angry at Charlotte Minto. He reached out to take her hands in his and tell her she should pay no never-mind to that stupid, self-centred hell-cat, but she backed away from him, shook her head, and gathering her shawl about her thin shoulders, turned and hurried away into the night.

5

BY the time Sam got bedded down, there wasn't much night left to speak of, which was just as well because sleep eluded him anyway. By first light, the settlers were up and getting their rigs ready for travel once more. By seven, Matt was riding the length of the line to make sure that everything was ready to go. Finally he spurred his pony up to the head of the column, where he was greeted by Reverend Berry.

"'Mornin', Reverend. You all set?"

Berry's broad smile was optimistic. "Indeed, Mr Dury, indeed. But where is Mr Judge this morning?"

"He's forged on ahead to find us a place to ford the river."

"Ah, very good. We are at your disposal, then, dear fellow. Lead on."

Matt hipped around in the saddle,

took one last look back along the canvas-topped line, then let out a strident yell. "*Yo-oo!*"

The column set off.

As he held his pony to a walk, Matt wondered what had happened to upset his partner, for *something* surely had. Sam had rolled out of his blankets long before anyone else that morning and growled something about going to hunt up a fording-place before tugging on his boots and going in search of his horse. Then there was the stiff formality he'd sensed in Mrs Minto when he'd stopped by to tip his hat to Rachel earlier, not to mention the careful way in which Jessica Berry had chosen to avoid his gaze.

There was no sign of Sam until about ten o'clock, at which time he came back down the trail at a canter. At once Matt called a halt, and as the order was relayed back down the line, Sam drew rein before the Berry Wagon.

He hadn't been sure what to expect

in the way of a reception from the preacher, but in the event it was quite cordial. "Good morning, Mr Judge," Berry said with a smile as he took off his hat to mop the shining dome beneath.

Sam nodded. "Reverend." He looked up at the preacher's sister, framed in the puckered canvas bow behind the schooner's seat. "Miss Berry."

Jessica could not even bring herself to look at him.

"You have found us a fording-place, Mr Judge?" Berry asked, peering up at him through travel-smeared spectacles.

Sam nodded again. "Uh-huh. About half a dozen miles further on."

"Will it be very dangerous?" Berry asked uncertainly.

"It'll be as safe as we can make it," Sam replied, dismounting. "I should say it'll be a little under half a mile from bank to bank, but we're in luck — the river runs shallow at that point. So, providin' we take it nice 'n' steady . . . " He stretched and reached for his canteen. "Reverend, I'd be obliged if you could choose me about a dozen men to take back out there with me. Them banks look sturdy enough to support these wagons, but it wouldn't do no harm to lay down some extry dirt an' brush to stop them from gettin' bogged."

"Of course, sir. I'll attend to it at once."

Sam took a pull from the canteen, swilled the water around to dislodge the dust in his mouth and spat off to the side. Matt watched him pat his pockets, searching for a cigar, heard him mutter a curse when he remembered he'd given his last two to the Cheyennes.

"You all right, Sam?" he asked tentatively, also stepping down.

Sam looked up. "Eh?"

"Somethin' botherin' you?"

Sam hooked his canteen back around the saddlehorn. "Should there be?" he asked testily.

Matt shrugged. Experience had taught him that you couldn't talk to Sam

123

when he was like this. The stubborn cuss . . . It was as well to let him get whatever it was out of his system in his own way, and at his own pace. "I guess not."

The older man busied himself checking his rig, then took off his hat and ran his fingers up through his thinning grey-black hair before setting the buff-coloured, round-crowned Stetson back atop his head. "Women," he muttered.

Matt glanced at him. "How's that again?"

"Aw, nothin'."

Matt eyed him a moment longer, then led his horse down to the river's-edge to drink. Sam watched him go, then strode across to the red-wheeled schooner and glanced up at the thin-faced woman on the seat, who was holding Mitzi in her arms and stroking the cat's head gently. "Miss Jessica," he said quietly.

She looked down at him; swiftly looked away again.

"I'm right sorry for what I did las' night," he said awkwardly. "Uhn . . . what I mean is, I'm not *sorry*. Not like how it sounds. Aw, heck . . . "

She looked down at him again and nodded to show that she understood what he was trying to say.

"That Charlotte Minto, she had no right sayin' what she did," he went on. "An' if you want to hear the truth ma'am . . . well, it wouldn't matter to me iffen you had three legs an' four eyes; I'd still consider myself real lucky to've knowed you."

Something moved in her eyes, and her uncertain smile turned even more trembly. She reached down one hand that he took and squeezed. "Well," he said, a bit embarrassed. "Just so long as you know."

A short while later, Berry returned with a dozen burly-looking men in tow, all of them either leading or riding huge draught-horses. "The extra hands you requested, Mr Judge," he said.

Sam headed back to his horse with a

brisk nod, all business once again. "All right, gents, let's move out. We got a lot of work to do before the first of these here wagons'll be ready to cross the river."

The Berry wagon didn't reach the spot Sam had chosen for the crossing until shortly after mid-day, by which time he and the other men had laid a kind of dirt and brush carpet upon which the iron-tyred wagons might grip as first they went into, then came out of, the eastward-flowing water. Berry stalled the oxen some yards away, and Sam came over to tell him that this was all going to take some time.

"Water's about five, six feet deep here, near as I can estimate," he explained, "but it may be a little deeper if the river-bed's got any trenches I ain't found yet. The current's not strong, but your people better double up their teams just to make sure they've got enough pullin'-power should they run into trouble."

Berry peered at the river. "I'll pass

the word," he said.

Soon a sort of picnic atmosphere had grown up around the stalled wagons that was far removed from the sheer hard toil going on down by the river as Berry's team was doubled up and Sam climbed aboard Charlie to lead the oxen slowly down into the cool water.

"Easy, now, easy," Sam muttered softly.

The oxen looked a little wide-eyed at first, but they soon settled down and were reasonably content so long as they could feel half-way solid ground under their hooves. They ploughed doggedly through the current with the schooner swaying and tilting slowly behind them.

The crossing was a slow and laborious business, but almost as soon as the Berry wagon started to press ahead, Matt led the second one down into the flow.

At last the first team of soaking oxen dragged the Berry wagon up onto the far bank and water swiftly puddled around the vehicle, turning the grass underfoot slippery. At once the men Sam had stationed over on the far side set about unyoking the spare oxen, turned them around and led them back through the water to be harnessed up to the next waiting wagon waiting in line.

And so it went on; slow, dangerous, back-breaking work, while the rest of the Easterners, for whom Sam had had little patience to begin with, treated the entire affair like a relaxed and pleasant excursion. Not that he could really blame them. This was a welcome respite from the monotony of the forced march, he guessed. But why couldn't they at least offer to *help*, 'stead of letting their many children run every which-way while they spread blankets and set out food or went to visit with their friends further down the line?

For the most part, the fording went without mishap. Then, along about three o'clock, one of the wagons located one of those trenches Sam had been worried about, and the vehicle slewed around and slowly began to capsize.

All at once the folks watching from both banks began to yell and scream, but Sam and Matt were already there plunging their mounts into the restless water yet again, closely followed by some of the other men, and after a time the wagon was hauled back upright, the folks inside checked for injuries, and the team urged on to complete the crossing in one battered, but otherwise unharmed, piece.

If nothing else, that little escapade served as an example to the rest of them that this *wasn't* a picnic, after all, and maybe they'd better start developing a healthy respect for what still lay ahead of them.

Slowly, slowly, each of the forty wagons was ferried across the steadily-flowing water. By the end of it, Sam, Matt and the burly-looking men with them were wet through and tired out. As evening approached, they dried off and changed clothes and went to find some grub before posting pickets and then bedding down for the night, but even then the day's excitement wasn't over. Shortly after ten o'clock that night, a woman's scream set the whole camp buzzing, but for only a while. It turned out that Mrs Spielmann was finally giving birth to her new baby boy, whom she would eventually decide to call Samuel.

* * *

Sam sent the hunters out right after church services next morning, it being the Sabbath, and the wagon train set off a couple of hours later, trekking northwest, away from the river, with the misty blue mountains shoving skyward still a hundred miles away.

Matt, taking up his usual position midway down the line, shortly found himself joined by Rachel, who had come out, ostensibly, to exercise her pony, Bonnie.

"Hello, Matt," the girl said as she urged her mount up alongside his.

The young Texan tipped his hat. "Rachel."

"I missed you this morning," the girl said. "When you didn't stop by to say hello, I mean."

Matt surveyed the line of rattling wagons, their cotton-twill coverings trembling and shaking to the lifts and dips of the trail. The morning was beginning to warm up pleasantly, the air to fill with the drone of horse-flies and the distant, sporadic popping of the hunters' guns. For as far as he could see in both directions, there was just a column of livestock and wagons, plodding men, crying children, grazing goats and slow-moving milk-cows.

"I didn't think it was a good idea," he replied at length. "Your mama, I suspicion she's taken a dislike to me."

"Oh, not to *you*," Rachel replied defensively.

He frowned. "To Sam, then, you mean? Why?"

Beneath her pea jacket, she shrugged. "I don't know. But she certainly hasn't been singing his praises to me the way she did a few days ago."

"Well, I sure can't deny that Sam's been actin' somewhat different himself, just lately," Matt replied. What he didn't say, though, was that, if anything, Sam's temper had *improved*, and that he was sure it had something to do with Reverend Berry's sour-faced sister — a revelation that would improve Charlotte Minto's humour not one whit should she get to hear of it.

"Mother says we should reach Spruce Valley within the fortnight," the girl said, changing the subject.

He nodded. "About that."

"I don't suppose we'll, ah . . . we'll be seeing each other for much longer, then."

His face clouded over, for she had given voice to something he had hitherto kept only as a depressing thought. "No," he replied quietly. "No, I don't guess we will."

132

"I'll miss you, Matt."

"Oh, we'll be around for a while yet," he said, putting a brave face on it. "Me 'n' Sam, we're kind of curious to see how this dream you folks've got works out."

"But once you've seen, you'll go, won't you?"

He reached over to cup her chin and bring her face up so that he could look into her sad blue eyes. "Hey, now," he said gently.

A flurry of gunshots sounded far off to the west, making them both face front abruptly. "What was that?" Rachel asked, alarmed.

He shook his head. "Not sure. But maybe I should go find out."

Up front, Sam had also heard the sudden burst of gunfire. At once he reined back and hauled his Spencer carbine from its sheath. As he worked the mechanism to put a .56 calibre bullet beneath the hammer, he wondered if they were about to meet the dreaded Django Reilly at last. He doubted that the gunfire would be anything to do with the Cheyennes, and — so far as he knew — the Sioux were further north, far beyond the North Platte River.

He stood up in the stirrups, squint-eyed, one hand raised to shield his vision from the bright sunlight above. The grassy flats stretched empty and serene ahead. Then his attention was taken by a movement over toward the left, as four riders burst out of the scant timber stippled there and started toward him in a ragged, hard-running line.

By now the wagon train was slowing to a stop and the emigrants were starting to ask each other what was going on. Sam recognised the approaching riders as the hunters he'd sent out earlier, knew from the reckless way they were pushing their mounts that they'd run into some kind of trouble for sure. One of them was slipping sideways in his saddle; now, as they came closer, Sam saw that the man's right shoulder was splashed with crimson.

Their pursuers burst out of the timber after them right then. There were three of them, white men, and they were using their spurs mercilessly to get as much speed out of their straining horses as they could. Sam heard them shouting, but couldn't tell if they were bawling a demand for the men ahead of them to stop or just giving voice to the savage fury combat always brought out in a feller.

Either way, they meant trouble, had already proved it by shooting one of the men he'd signed on to protect, and if he didn't take a hand soon, the situation was only likely to get worse.

He heard Matt ride up behind him, turned, saw Rachel right beside him. Over by his wagon, Reverend Berry called a question, but there was no time to answer it. *"Stay here!"* he barked, and as Matt nodded, he kicked Charlie into a gallop.

He pushed the roan as hard as he dared, aware that neither of them were getting any younger, saw now that one of the hunters had steered his horse in close to that of the wounded man, was reaching across to steady him in the saddle. Sam raised the Spencer, used it to wave them on, then swung out and around them so that he could form some kind of barrier between them and the men who meant to do them harm.

He focused his attention on those varmints now. He could see them clearer than before. They didn't look like the kind of trail-scum he'd expect to find riding with Reilly. Neither could he really imagine the Mexican-Irish owlhoot picking such open country in which to try robbing his train. Hell, these fellers, they were decked out in range-gear. Their big spurs, coiled lariats and small, wiry horses pegged them as rangemen.

One of them had thrust out ahead of the others. He held a big pistol in one hand while he used the other to saw at the reins and draw even more speed from his lathered mount. The sonofabitch — obviously no respecter of horses — was in his middle-thirties, with a hard, tanned face screwed up into a killer's mask. His hard brown eyes were lit up with rage, his nostrils flared, his thick lips drawn down into a snarl that allowed the sunlight to sparkle off his big, square teeth.

The man from Texas realised at last that the two men in back of the lead-rider were urging him to slow down and give up the chase, but he was choosing to ignore them.

He fired his handgun again; once more; a third time. His shots went wide of the mark, were likely triggered more for effect than anything else. Still, if he was allowed to carry on like that, someone was going to get hurt.

Taking a leaf out of the Cheyennes' book, Sam used knee pressure to turn his racing roan onto a course that would intercept the ornery oncomer. He brought the Spencer back up and started waving it again, but this time the message he was trying to send out was for the other man to haul down before they collided.

Instead, the other man extended his handgun to arms'-length and squeezed the trigger again.

It was doubtful that he'd hit much, of course, seated aboard a hurricane deck as he was, but even so, it was real lucky for Sam that the other man had used up all his bullets, and that the hammer came down on an empty casing.

There was no time to appreciate the fact, though. Sam's roan and the other man's pony had been eating up ground at a startling rate; now they were bearing down on each other at a wall-eyed gallop, too close to pull away even had their riders so wished.

Moments later the horses collided with a solid, painful whack and Charlie staggered a bit edgewise while the other man's pony bounced off the heavier animal and crashed sideways, momentarily dazed.

The horse landed hard in the tall

grass and its rider came out of the stirrups like a veteran. His grey hat went sailing one way as he went blundering in the other. He fell, rolled, cursed, came up searching for his fallen gun.

His pony leapt back up then, and he lunged for the rifle jutting from the sheath on the near side.

By then, though, Sam had climbed down from his own horse and was covering him with the cocked carbine. He brought the Spencer up to his shoulder as he snapped, "Hold it, son! I mean it! Touch that saddlegun an' I'll burn you from belly to backbone!"

The younger man froze, breathing hard, sweaty and red-faced, his brown eyes fierce beneath a scowl and his fine blond hair a wild tangle down over his ears and forehead. He wore a yellow bandanna at his throat. His white shirt was tucked into turned-up jeans and worn beneath a buttoned-up grey vest. He wore his holster high; the gun he'd lost in the tall grass had been a blued Peacemaker.

They glared at each other, both men panting, neither one ready to back down, until the blond man's two companions came up aboard heaving mounts. Then Sam took a step back and around, so that he could keep all three of them covered.

"That's about far enough, fellers," he said grimly, gesturing with the Spencer to punch his words home. "Now toss them guns aside."

The blond man's companions were of an age with him, perhaps a few years younger. The feller on the left was loose-limbed and lanky, with a thick moustache blending into the five-day stubble coating his pointed jaw. The rider to his right looked some smarter, with a softer, clean-shaven face, short brown hair and clear, concerned brown eyes.

"Don't listen to him!" barked the blond man.

But the feller with the concerned brown eyes said, "Aw, shut up, Dean. There's no point making a mountain out of a molehill."

The blond man, Dean, said, "I don't think your pappy'll see it that way, Jim. Man rustles McCandish stock, we make 'im pay the price!"

Sam frowned. "Why don't you jus' back up a minute, Dean? What's all this talk about rustlin'?" he demanded.

Dean jerked his chin in the direction the hunters had taken, back to the wagon train a few hundred yards to the northeast. "You know well enough," he said. "Else you wouldn't've been so quick to defend 'em."

Sam sighed. "Maybe one o' you other fellers'd care to explain what this here galoot refuses to tell me," he invited.

Before either man could speak, a second bunch of riders came out of the distant timber with a giant of a man at their head, and Sam felt his stomach clench. Three-to-one odds he could just about handle. Eleven-to-one would require a little more effort than he could comfortably give.

Almost simultaneously, however, he heard the drumming of more horse-hooves coming from behind him, and the three cowboys focused warily on the arrival of his own reinforcements as Matt and Rachel came upon the scene, Matt holding his Winchester loosely across his lap.

"You got some trouble here, Sam?" Matt asked tightly.

"Well, I got me three feather-brains who say we been rustlin' their stock," Sam replied. "An' a little extry company just yonder."

By now the second group of horsemen were nearly upon them. They were a hard-looking crew and they were fairly bristling with weapons. But Dean seemed oblivious to their approach. One kind of fire had replaced another in his eyes as he studied Rachel brazenly. He reached up to palm his hair back off his face and a slow, easy grin spread across his mouth. "Well, now," he said with a low whistle. "Look what we got here."

At last the weapon-heavy horsemen drew rein and the man at their head — tall, weathered, fiftyish, with a round, florid face and cropped, snow-white hair — raked his brown eyes across the scene, taking in the situation and trying to make sense out of it all.

He raised his left hand, signalling the crew behind him to stay where they were, while he himself walked his sorrel closer. He was a heavy man, big-bellied but strong with it. He wore a grey four-finger pinch atop his head, a blue cotton shirt, worn jeans and low-heeled, spurless boots. High about his waist was buckled a Colt in .38 calibre.

"What's goin' on here?" he snapped.

The feller with the concerned brown eyes, Jim McCandish, said, "Pa, this — "

The elder McCandish cut across him, addressing Dean. Sam, Matt and Rachel might just as well have been invisible for all the attention he paid them. "Mike?" he prodded.

Dean finally prised his eyes from Rachel in order to throw a murderous look at Sam. "We were out huntin' up strays on the south quarter," he said. "Heard gunfire, went to take a look-see."

"And?" said McCandish.

Sam felt something cold and heavy settle in his stomach. Suddenly he thought he could guess what was coming, what this whole business had been about, and again he found himself cursing the stupidity of these damned Easterners.

"Saw four fellers crowded round a yearling they'd just shot dead," Mike Dean went on. "Looked to me like they was fixin' to rope her an' drag her away, so I shot at one of 'em, winged 'im, I think, then me an' Jim an' Ben here, we come after 'em. Would've caught 'em, too, but for this old feller. He knocked me outta my saddle, then forced Jim an' Ben to throw down their guns."

McCandish pondered that for a

moment. His tough face was immobile. At last his hard brown eyes swivelled to burn into Sam. "That right, mister?" he asked.

"It's right that I sent four men out this mornin' to see what they could pot for supper," Sam replied. "It's possible that they spied one o' your cows, an' bein' know-nothin' greenhorns, shot her dead, in which case you'll have to take my word for it that there was no intention to knowin'ly steal from you. As for your man there shootin' one of our people — that's right, too. Caught him in the right shoulder."

"You're not denyin' any of it, then?" said McCandish.

"Only the part about me bein' old," Sam replied solemnly.

McCandish moved his gaze a fraction, to look over Sam's shoulder at the stalled wagon train. He was weighing the evidence, trying to decide if the emigrants could really have been so stupid. At last he said, "You got any doctors with yonder train, mister?"

Sam nodded. "A couple."

"You ought to be able to get your wounded man patched up all right, then — in which case, they's no real harm done, I guess."

"Mr McCandish — !" Dean began indignantly.

McCandish glanced at him. "Go find your piece, Mike, then get back to work. Same goes for you others. I'll be along directly."

But Dean stayed right where he was, and for a while there it looked as if he would disregard his employer's orders, go ahead and make something more out of it and to hell with the consequences.

"Mike . . ."

But then Dean's eyes shifted back to Rachel, and again something sly, bold and unpleasant entered his gaze. He reached down to pick up his hat, not once taking his eyes off her, seemingly unaware of just how his attentions made her skin crawl. He grinned up at her, insolent and brazen, said, "Hope to see you again sometime, little missy."

Matt made a warning sound in his throat but somehow held himself on a short rein until Dean turned, found his gun, stuffed it away and remounted.

McCandish watched him join the others, followed their progress as they wheeled their mounts and headed back the way they'd come, then swung down from the sorrel, a bear of a man, and came over with his right hand extended. "It's Judge, isn't it? Saw you keepin' the peace one time down in Hays City, you an' Hickok."

Sam was surprised. "Hell, mister, you've got a good memory. That was twelve, thirteen years ago."

"Never forget a face, though. The name's McCandish, Judge. Tom McCandish. I own all the land to the south an' west of here. Be obliged iffen you'd keep your people off it for as long as you're in the neighbourhood."

Sam nodded and shook with him, relaxing a touch now that the confrontation had passed. "I'll do that," he replied. "But maybe you'd ought to post some signs in future, McCandish, an' fence your property off."

The rancher turned his attention to Matt and Rachel, and after Sam did the honours and the two younger people turned their horses back to the train, McCandish said, "You'll have to make allowances for Mike Dean, Judge. He's a good foreman, the best. But he can be a hot-head sometimes, 'specially where the TM Connected's concerned."

"Your son seemed like a nice feller," Sam remarked.

"Jim?" McCandish shrugged his massive shoulders. "Aw, Jim's all right, I guess. But he favours his mother. You know, book-readin' an' the like." The way he said it made it sound like a sin. "To be honest with you, Judge, there's times I think Jim could learn a thing or two from Mike Dean. Tenacity, for one. Man's got to have tenacity to hold onto anythin' out here. Got to be stubborn and ruthless.

But Jim . . . hell, he'd sooner pick up a book an' wear his eyes out."

The rancher took off his hat and mopped his hairless pate. "This your line of work now, is it?" he asked. "Guidin' greenhorns to the Promised Land?"

"More what you'd call a temporary position," Sam replied.

"Well, they's some good country about ten miles further down the trail your people might care to camp on. That steer your hunters killed, it's just the other side of that timber. You want to send someone over to butcher it an' pack it out, you're welcome. But don't let it happen again, Judge. I can be a forgivin' man, up to a point."

Sam read the threat in the other man's voice, but chose to ignore it for reasons of diplomacy. "Thanks, McCandish. 'Preciate it. Oh, by the way . . . "

The cattleman halted in the process of toeing into the stirrup. "Yeah?"

"Name Django Reilly mean anythin'

to you?" Sam asked.

McCandish worked up some spit and let it go in a silvery stream. "Now there *is* a sonofabitch," he said. "Nothin's too low for that skunk, way I hear it. Been cuttin' up somethin' shameful in these parts of late, killin' an' robbin' an' the like. But he knows better'n to make trouble with the TM. He leaves us alone, we leave him alone. Why? You had trouble with him yourself?"

Sam shook his head. "Not yet. But you know somethin'? I got the damnedest feelin' it's only a matter of time before we do."

6

THEY did as Tom McCandish had suggested and continued on westward into the dying afternoon until, some ten miles later, they came to a wide area of grassy parkland that offered wood, graze and water, and there Sam called a halt and set about getting the emigrants settled in for the night.

Darkness fell softly, like purple powder drifting down from the heavens to steal the blue from the sky. The men Sam had sent out to cut up and fetch in the dead steer came in a short time later and soon the sweet smell of freshly-cooked meat began to spice up the cool evening air.

At last Sam felt some of the day's tension leave him. The Cheyennes were behind them. The trouble with Tom McCandish had been averted. But there

151

was still Reilly to consider, so Sam took a turn around the perimeter to check on the pickets before going off to break bread with Cyrus Kennedy, who had extended the invitation to him and Matt earlier that day.

He paused a while before heading for Kennedy's wagon, enjoying the peace and tranquillity of dusk. Around them, the land was quiet, empty, immense. There was a time when men had called this 'Unorganised Territory', and not so very long ago, either. But there was precious little left of the untamed wilderness now, he thought. He remembered the country as it had been in his youth, raw and dangerous and exciting. It could still be all three, of course, but sometimes, surrounded by the trappings of civilisation, a man tended to forget that and imagine himself as some kind of leftover from a past age, a dinosaur perhaps, with no place in the modern world.

Ah, but out here, here where there was hardly any such thing as civilisation, just simple folk with honest aims, it was easier to recall the old days. And for the first time, as darkness thickened from the east and settled around him, Sam began to realize that perhaps that was why these people were risking everything to reach Spruce Valley; to get *away* from the rest of mankind, the ugly side of it, at any rate. If that was the case, then he concluded that maybe they weren't so dumb after all.

By the time he reached Kennedy's wagon, Matt was already there waiting for him. They dined on plain fare and spoke of the journey, the many Kennedy children, Galveston Jones, the other emigrants. It was peaceful and pleasant until sometime around eight o'clock, when one of the pickets came in from the south side of the camp and trotted over with an ancient but serviceable rifle held across his chest and a worried look on his square, ruddy face.

Sam and Matt had already seen him coming, of course, and by the time he reached them, they were on their feet, awaiting his arrival. "What's the problem, Haas?" Sam asked when he was near enough.

The German hooked a thumb over his shoulder. "There iss a rider coming in, Mr Judge."

"Just the one?"

"So far ass I coult see."

Sam nodded. He opened his mouth to ask Haas whether or not the newcomer had been riding a shod horse, which would at least give them some indication as to whether he was a red man or white, then checked himself, certain that the German would not have known the difference, even if he'd thought to listen out for it. "All right," he said instead. "Let's go take a look-see who it is and find out what he wants." He turned to Kennedy's wife and tipped his hat. "Thank you for the meal, ma'am. Now, if you'll pardon us . . . "

They followed the picket back over towards the line of wagons that formed the south side of camp. It was largely quiet now. Most of the emigrants had long-since bedded down, although a few were still gathered here and there, conversing in low tones. Moonlight whitened the canvas coverings. Small campfires and the odd crackling faggot etched the immediate area in shades of red and saffron. Beyond the circle of wagons, however, the prairie was pitch-dark, and grave-silent.

By the time they reached the gap between one wagon and the next and climbed over the sloping tongue, it became obvious that their visitor had already drawn in under the watchful, suspicious eyes of two other pickets, who were keeping him covered with their long guns. He sat his horse calmly, gloved hands folded atop the saddlehorn. He was clean-shaven, so far as they could see in the weak light, dressed like a rangeman in cuffed jeans and a buttoned-to-the-neck denim jacket. Furthermore, he was unarmed save for a saddlegun in a sheath under the off-side fender.

When Sam and Matt came to a halt before him, the rider reached up slowly and tugged at his wide-brimmed brown hat. "I'm sorry if I'm intruding, Mr Judge," he said. "But I'd appreciate a few words, if that's all right."

Sam narrowed his gaze, recognising the voice. Squinting up at the rider he said, "It's Jim McCandish, ain't it?"

"Yes sir."

Sam didn't know much about the rancher's son other than what he'd seen of him earlier and what Tom McCandish himself had said about him, but the young man had struck him as a straight-shooter, so he told the pickets to put up their guns and go back to their positions, then said, "Climb down an' share some coffee with us, son."

As he swung down, Jim said, "Obliged to you," and leading his horse by its reins, he followed Sam and Matt back into the circle of light, tied his animal to the nearest wagon-wheel and loosened his girth, then stamped across to the central fire, where a bucket of coffee was always cooking for the men patrolling the perimeter through the long darkness hours. His arrival caused a mild stir of interest among the settlers who were still awake to see it, but as Sam took a mug, dipped it into the brew and passed it across, and asked him what brought him out this way, he kept his voice confidential.

Jim McCandish took the mug and cupped his hands around it to warm them through, for the night was sharp. Steam rose off it in a series of grey curls. He looked very serious and not a little awkward as he said, "Well, it's about Mike Dean."

"Dean?" said Matt, helping himself to coffee. "Your pa's foreman?"

Jim nodded. "He hasn't been by here at all tonight, I suppose?"

"No," said Sam. "Should he have?"

The young man took a pull at the coffee to delay his reply. He was in his mid-twenties, though he appeared much younger, partially because of his obvious naivete, partly because the outdoor life had yet to leave any real impression upon him. "To be honest, Mr Judge, I'm not sure. We were over at Corby's place earlier tonight — that's a kind of trading post that doubles as a watering-hole, about twelve miles due south. The hands always go out there on a Sunday night and pa likes me to tag along with 'em. I guess he figures that sooner or later it'll make a man out of me." He gave a self-conscious twitch of a smile and his voice, in that moment, held much irony. "Anyway, Mike was still feeling sore about what happened earlier this afternoon, and it looked to me like he was out to get mean-drunk. I've seen it before, so I know all the signs. Anyway, pretty soon he started talking about . . . "

"Go on, son," Sam prodded when the rancher's boy fell silent.

"Well, he started saying things about that young girl who was out there on the plains with you today."

Matt was immediately on the defensive. "Rachel?" he said.

Jim nodded. "If that's her name." He said, "Well, you can guess what line they took. Eventually he staggered outside, to relieve himself, or so I thought. But when he didn't come back after a time I went out to look for him. He'd quit Corby's."

"And you thought he'd come here? To pester Rachel?"

Jim shrugged. "Mike's a mean enough cuss when he's sober. In his cups, there's no meaner sonofabitch on the face of this earth."

Sam threw a look out into the cloaking shadows. "Maybe he went back to your pappy's place to sleep it off. You said he was staggerin'."

"Maybe. But — "

It was about then that Reverend Berry came over to them, the innocuous blue eyes behind his spectacles showing some concern as he regarded their visitor. "Good evening, Mr, ah . . . ?"

"This is Jim McCandish from the

TM Connected, reverend," said Sam. Briefly he explained why Jim had stopped by.

"Oh dear," said Berry, beginning to fluster. "You don't *really* believe that this man Dean means us some sort of malice, do you, Mr McCandish?"

"Probably not, pastor," Jim replied, finishing his coffee and setting his mug down. "But Mike's got a nasty reputation for toting grudges, so I thought the least I could do was warn you, just in case."

"We're grateful to you, sir."

"Well, I guess I'd best be getting along. Thanks for the coffee, Mr Judge."

"Thanks for the warnin'," Sam replied.

They were just about to turn and go back over to Jim's horse when a voice came out of the darkness at them, slurred, deep, mean, undeniably Mike Dean's.

" . . . Hello the camp . . . "

They froze. Sam felt Jim's gaze on

him as the muscles around his eyes and mouth tightened. Jim said, "Dammit, I was right! He *did* figure to come out here and make trouble for you!"

To keep the situation from getting out of hand, Sam said, "We don't know that for a fact, gents." But even as he said it, he knew it was just wishful thinking.

"Here, I'll go try to talk some sense into him," Jim offered, but before he could move, Dean walked his cow-pony in through the gap between the wagons and, after a brief glance around, headed directly for the fire at the centre of the camp. He looked much the same as he had earlier that day, with his white shirt worn under a buttoned-up grey vest and a holster filled with Peacemaker riding high around the waistband of his jeans. He came on at a slow pace as they spread out on the far side of the fire, with its battered bucket of black coffee spewing out a wall of steam to separate them, and gradually the shadows hiding his face began to recede until they could all make out his hard brown eyes, the belligerent flare of his nostrils, the looseness of the lips hiding his big, square teeth. His eyes had a watery look to them, Sam saw as he came nearer, watery and bloodshot, and high colour smudged his cheeks. He was liquored-up, all right, just as Jim McCandish had said he would be.

Dean drew in about a dozen feet away. Most of the emigrants had climbed to their feet and stood watching him in tense, expectant silence. He looked vaguely surprised to find Jim McCandish among their number, but he recovered quickly enough and a slow, insolent grin bloomed on his lips.

"Evenin'," he said sociably.

Sam replied. "Evenin', Dean. You out takin' the fresh air, are you?"

"Come to pay my respects," Dean slurred.

"Oh?"

"Uh-huh. To that there pretty little missy I spied with you-all this afternoon."

Sam said, "It's late, Dean. She'll be a-bed by now."

The foreman's grin grew lewd and ugly. "An' that's where I figure she'd do the most good," he answered with a low chuckle.

Matt stiffened, jaw muscles working, and to defuse an increasingly dangerous situation, Sam said, "Have a little respect, Mike. An' show a little sense. Why don't you jus' turn around an' be on your way afore you wake her up, huh?"

Dean actually appeared to consider the suggestion. The only sound was the crackle of the fire. But at the end of a long, slow thirty seconds, he shook his head. "Naw. I come all this way . . . " He climbed down, left his horse ground-hitched and glanced around at the surrounding wagons, ignoring the curious faces regarding him fearfully in return. "Hey, little missy!" he called out. "Where you hidin' at, huh?"

Somewhere in one of the wagons, a

disturbed baby began to cry.

"For God's sake, Mike!" said Jim McCandish. "Get on back to the ranch!"

Dean spun, swift as a snake, and stabbed him with a murderous glare. "The day you give me orders hasn't dawned yet, Jim!" he hissed.

To his credit, Jim stood his ground. "When my pa hears about this — "

"Your pa lets me do any damn' thing I please," Dean replied. "An' you know it."

"Uh, Mr Dean . . . " It was Reverend Berry. "Why don't we all just calm down and share coffee?"

"'Cause I'm kind of particular about who I share coffee with, pastor," Dean replied acidly. "And I'd as soon not share it with you folks."

"Perhaps you'd better just get back aboard that horse and head on out of here then," suggested Matt.

Dean grinned a challenge at him. "An' you're the man to make me?"

"If needs be."

"Whoo-boy! Ambitious cuss, ain't you?"

Sam took a pace around the fire. "Dean — "

Dean jabbed a finger at him. His face appeared even more flushed in the uneven fire-splash than it had when he'd first arrived, and he was swaying ever so slightly. "You can stay out of this too, old-timer! I still got a score to settle with you for this afternoon." He took another look around the camp. "Hey, now, little missy, come on out here where I can see yuh! Come on! Ol' Mike's come to spark yuh!"

"You're drunk, Mike," Jim McCandish said in disgust.

There was a movement away someplace on the eastern edge of the camp and as all eyes turned that way, Rachel Minto and her mother climbed down out of their wagon, wrapped in ankle-length dressing-gowns and clutching shawls about their shoulders, their faces orange ovals of disquiet and apprehension.

"Mr Dean," Charlotte said in a voice that was struggling to remain even and calm and totally in command. "My . . . my daughter and I will thank you to leave now. We do not wish to entertain you, and would as soon you left us be."

With effort, Mike Dean pulled them both into focus; then, disregarding Charlotte, he sharpened his gaze specifically upon the younger redhead. His left hand came up and he rubbed at his jaw, his earlier swagger intensified now, and the thoughts running through his head at that moment all too plain to read in his expression. He bobbed his head and said, "Evenin' there, little missy . . . "

He started over there and Charlotte put a protective arm around her daughter. Matt looked across at them, mother and child, and decided that this business had gone far enough. "All right, Dean," he said sharply, going around the fire on a course that would block the other man. "You came to see the girl. You've seen her. Now — "

Dean tossed a scowl at him. His hard brown eyes were hot and threatening. "Butt out of this, boy," he growled. Then he continued on across to the girl who had so fired his lust, remorseless, muttering obscene suggestions that made Rachel tremble.

Matt went after him fast, closed the gap between them, and just as realization dawned in Dean's mind that he hadn't intimidated this tall, double gun-hung man the way he had always intimidated just about everyone else, Matt was upon him with a lunge, left hand grabbing a shoulder full of shirt, bunched right fist coming in fast to punch him in the stomach.

A kind of collective gasp went through the hushed watchers then, and later Matt thought he heard Rachel scream his name. But the next few moments became more difficult to recall with any degree of certainty.

Dean took the blow and went backwards with it, partly in surprise, partly in order to lessen its impact. He was a veteran of the bunkhouse brawl, that was likely how he'd worked his way up to tophand, and he recovered fast and came in with his temper up and both his own fists hammering away like pistons. It became Matt's turn to fall victim to surprise and back up under this fresh onslaught, for Dean had a weight advantage over his opponent and he had more experience, too, and damned if he wasn't going to use them both to the full.

Mike Dean's vicious roundhouse right caught him aside the head and rocked him sideways. He went back a few paces, came so close to the fire that he actually felt the heat of it against his calves, then blocked another punch, took one more in the midriff, somehow fought to reach through Dean's guard and shove him off again.

That gave them both a bit of a breather, a brief moment to stand back, consider tactics and then put them into action. Dean shook his head to clear it, sprayed blood from his nose in a fine mist that sizzled in the fire. Matt cuffed blood from his swollen top lip. Reverend Berry cleared his throat, opened his mouth and managed to say, "Gentlemen, please — ", but by then the lull was over and they were going at each other again, the reason for the fight temporarily forgotten, each man heedless of possible injury and wanting only to incapacitate the other.

Matt swung a right cross. Dean dodged away from it. Dean came in with a right to Matt's belly that lifted the Texan up onto his toes, followed through with a left, one more right that pushed Matt back again.

He made a mistake then, he came forward and flung his right leg out, intending to catch Matt in the groin, but Matt kept going backwards so that he was out of reach of the kick, but not so far out of reach that he couldn't grab hold of that pointed, spur-hung boot and twist hard so that Dean yelled from the pain in his ankle and staggered backwards, arms windmilling, off balance.

Dean stumbled, came up against his horse, and the animal sidestepped away from him, wall-eyed and wary. Dean came forward again wearing a scowl, dancing light on his feet, fists moving and shifting all the time. Someone screamed, "Stop them, somebody! For God's sake, stop them!" and that was just what Sam wanted to do, but Matt was already going in again, throwing caution to the wind, shoving his man again to keep him off-balance, snapping his head sideways with a right cross, whipping it the other way with a left, always pushing him back, back, seeing that ugly, smudged, bruised, blood-streaked face only as a target for his now-raw knuckles.

Then the young Texan saw something go out in Dean's eyes, and he realised that the fight was as good as over. He hit Dean one last time and Dean spilled over backwards and skidded a little way on the slick grass, rolled onto his side, breathing hard.

Matt stood a few yards away from him, spread-legged, shoulders hunched, fighting to regain his own breath. Around them, the camp was silent save for the baby that was still bawling.

"Now . . . get on your . . . horse and . . . get out . . . of here, Dean . . . " Matt panted, working up some spit to clear his mouth.

Dean glared up at him through those hard, bloodshot hazel eyes, his face so much mincemeat. He rolled onto his belly, pushed himself up onto his knees, hatless now, fine blond hair awry. Matt began to turn away from him, figuring to go clean up and examine the extent of his injuries, and that was why he didn't see Dean rise up suddenly, claw for the Peacemaker on his hip, didn't know anything about the foreman's attempt at treachery until Rachel screamed his name again.

Then instinct took command, told him what was happening, and he spun back around to confirm it with his eyes, forcing his stinging hands to swoop down towards the grips of his Tranters, haul iron, lift, aim, fire —

Dean was up on his feet and his .45 was just clearing leather when gun-thunder shattered the tension of the moment and Matt's bullets hit him in the chest, slapping dust from his grey vest and pulling streamers of blood from out of the two ragged holes that suddenly erupted in the material. Dean hunched up under the impacting slugs, his face screwed up still further. He pulled the trigger of his own gun and it discharged into the ground, kicking up a divot of earth. Then Dean went around and down, almost gracefully, and measured his length on the grass, where he began to twist and writhe like a snake on a chopping block.

Matt stood exactly where he was, Tranters wisping smoke up into the cool night air, shocked by what he had done, what he had been forced to do. On the ground Dean clutched his shattered chest and husked, "Jesus, I'm killed . . . "

That broke the spell. A few of the assembled women began to moan or sob. Sam and the reverend hustled over to the fallen man, Sam to inspect the damage and Berry to take the foreman's cold hands and offer something in the way of spiritual comfort.

With a struggle Jim McCandish finally managed to tear his eyes away from the dying man and went over to Matt. "You . . . you had no choice, Dury," he said quietly, his voice dry and quivery, his face pale. He put a hand on Matt's shoulder, but Matt made no move to acknowledge him. He was stunned. How could this fine and peaceful evening have ended in his killing a man? He shook his head, unable to comprehend it.

One of the train's two doctors appeared, a tall, angular man with greying temples and an old brown leather case that rattled with surgical irons. He knelt beside Dean and gently prised his hands away from his chest.

"I'm killed . . . " Dean muttered again, shivering.

They were the last two words he ever said.

The doctor sighed audibly. "He's gone," he said.

Sam's shoulders sagged, for there was little to enjoy in watching a man die. He took his hat off and batted it against his thigh, fighting down his rising irritation, then ran his fingers up through his hair and clapped the hat back down, longing more than ever for a cigar and wishing he hadn't been so free with them before.

Jim McCandish said, "You'd better get your people the hell out of here, Mr Judge."

Sam glanced at him sharply. "How's that again?"

"My pa's not going to be best pleased about this."

"*I'm* not best pleased about it."

"But there's a difference. My father will make you pay for it if you stay here," Jim pointed out. "He'll make every last one of you pay."

Sam closed the distance towards him. Matt, coming out of his stupor, put his guns away and joined them, as did Reverend Berry and Charlotte and Rachel Minto. "Maybe you'd better explain just what it is you're tryin' to say, Jim," Sam invited in a soft, dangerous voice. "Mike Dean brought this on himself. You're makin' it sound as if Matt killed him deliberate."

"I know exactly what happened," Jim said grimly, "and you can rely on me to tell it straight. But Mike Dean was . . . well, he was more like one of the family, at least so far as my pa was concerned. What Mike said just now about my pa letting him do whatever he liked was true. Mike was the kind of man my pa wanted me to be. Sometimes I think he *was* more of a son than I am." He looked from Sam to Matt, from Matt to the others, then returned his concerned brown eyes to Sam's lean, weathered visage. "He's going to want revenge for Mike's death, Mr Judge," he said earnestly. "Do you understand me? He's not going to want to know the rights and wrongs of it. That's not my father's way. He's just going to want to make you pay. *All* of you."

"Then maybe I'd better dissuade him from the notion," Sam said pensively.

"I'll go," Matt cut in. "It was me who burned Dean down, don't forget."

"He'll string you up, Dury," Jim warned him gravely.

"That's a chance I'll have to take."

"And what about all these other people?"

Charlotte frowned. "He'd leave them alone, surely?"

Jim shook his head. "I honestly don't know, ma'am."

"I'll be damned if I'll run from what I've done," said Matt.

"Then you're a fool. Believe me, I *know* my father."

Sam turned away from the group, pursing his lips. He recalled the glint in

Tom McCandish's eye that afternoon when he'd said he could be a forgiving man, up to a point. And it was true that the big rancher *had* thought a lot of Dean.

"I can't run from this, Sam," Matt said from behind him. "But neither do I want to put the rest of these people in any danger."

Sam turned back to him. "Then what do you suggest?"

Matt ran his tongue across his lips. His face appeared to have been hewn from granite. "That you move out tonight, get the train to hell and gone from here, while I ride out to the TM Connected with Jim and tell McCandish exactly what happened."

While Sam considered this, Jim McCandish said, "I think you're a fool, Dury. You don't know my father. But if you're so dead-set on it . . . "

"I am."

"All right. But I'll warn you one last time. There's no law out here save McCandish Law. And even if there was, my pa would still be a law unto himself."

Sam's sigh was weighty. It wasn't exactly an ideal situation, but he couldn't come up with anything better. To run from a killing was as good as confessing your guilt in the matter, and Matt had only acted in defence of his life. It was as well to get the business settled before it got out of control, else it could hound him the rest of his days. Still, he couldn't help but remember Jim's warning, and it made apprehension stir deep in his gut.

Reaching a decision at last he said wearily, "Reverend, get your people ready to move out."

"But . . . they are exhausted, Mr Judge."

"We all are, reverend. But we'll find 'em some time to rest up tomorrow. For now, young McCandish here is right; the further you are from this place, the less likely you are to be drawn into any trouble that might follow."

There was no arguing with that, so the priest hustled away to call the stunned and horrified spectators together and explain exactly what it was they were fixing to do.

Matt let out a long breath and regarded his boots. The killing had left him feeling hollow. It always did, no matter how much the other feller might have had it coming. He felt a cool palm on his forearm and looked around.

Charlotte Minto looked up into his very serious face and said quietly, "Thank you for what you did to protect my daughter, Mr Dury. I know how much it has affected you. But . . . if it is any consolation, I believe you had right on your side."

"Thank you, ma'am," he said mechanically.

"Matt . . . " said Rachel.

"It'll be all right," he assured her.

Charlotte led the girl away just as Reverend Berry's sister came up with Mitzi slinking along at her heels.

Wordlessly she handed Sam a folded blanket. He knew what it was for and nodded his thanks. When Matt went off to catch up his horse and prepare for travel, he and Jim McCandish rolled the dead man into the blanket, hoisted him up over his saddle, and when they got him balanced just right, tied him into place.

Again Sam felt a stirring of disquiet. God help Tom McCandish if he failed to give Matt a fair hearing, he thought. If the rancher did anything to harm his son, then by Christ Sam would settle with him quickly, violently — and permanently.

7

THEY sat their horses right there, where it had happened, and watched the wagon train rock and rattle ponderously away to the west, each man alone with his thoughts. Jim McCandish held the reins to the death-horse, which stood between them, uneasy with its grisly burden. A cool breeze blew up, chilling their skin and making their horses' ears twitch. The wagons vanished like a ghostly procession beneath the white moonshine. After a while Matt felt Jim's eyes upon him and hipped around to face him.

"Ready?" the younger McCandish asked.

Matt nodded. "I guess."

They turned their mounts toward the southwest and set off at a walk. Jim said that his father's place lay about fifteen miles that way, but neither man was in any hurry to reach it. If Tom McCandish was going to take the news of his foreman's death the way Jim had predicted, then Matt wanted to buy the train as much time as he could to make tracks out of there.

The night was starry and vast. The prairie was open, flat for the most part, but occasionally it rose in sweeping, brush-littered swells, and here and there rose bosques of shadow-thick timber. The riding was easy, and required little concentration, which was just as well, for each man had plenty enough to occupy him as it was.

They came within sight of the ranch at about ten o'clock. The place was largely in darkness. The day started early out here, and likely finished early too, save for when the hired hands went drinking at this place Corby's, as they had tonight. But the windows of the main house were filled with lamplight, so someone was still awake.

They rode in at a walk. Matt looked

around him, getting the measure of the place. The ranch appeared to be well maintained and orderly in the darkness. The dirt yard was bordered by a long, narrow bunkhouse and a large barn, stable and corral. Right next to the stable he identified a blacksmith's shop, and tacked onto the end of the bunkhouse was a cookshack with a high stone chimney. Cattle-sounds floated in from the surrounding pastures, along with the occasional snatch of some nighthawk's lonely shanty.

They reined in before the main house, a sprawling, single-storey log-built structure with a shingled roof and an air of sturdy permanence. Flowers grew abundantly in rows out front and in little hanging baskets to either side of the front door — the work of Mrs McCandish, Matt felt sure.

There must have been something about their slow, funereal entrance that had attracted the people inside. Either that or someone in there had seen them coming and spied the body they were leading along behind them. Whichever, by the time they drew in, the front door had been opened and Tom McCandish, big-bellied, dressed in creased range-garb, hatless but carrying a Winchester across his barrel chest, stood watching their arrival, and beside him stood a small, still-beautiful woman in a neck-high gingham dress, late forties, early fifties, with a small, pleasant face, dark hair centre-parted and gathered in buns to either side of her head. The woman had one tiny fist held up to her mouth.

"Jim?" she said when they were near enough. She had a light, contralto voice. Matt heard the worry in it clearly through the shadows.

"I'm all right, ma," Jim replied.

Ignoring his son, Tom McCandish held Matt's eyes with his own. He nodded a cautious greeting, then gestured to the body with the barrel of the Winchester. "Trouble?" he asked carefully.

"Your foreman," Matt replied.

McCandish's wife gasped. "He came out to our camp a couple of hours ago, figuring to see a girl who didn't want to see him. We asked him to leave. He wouldn't. There was a fight. He went for his gun. I killed him."

McCandish's wife made another small sound in her throat. McCandish himself only said, "A fight?"

Matt nodded.

"A gunfight?" the rancher persisted. A couple of hired men, clearly disturbed from sleep by their voices, came out of the bunkhouse to see what was going on.

"A fist-fight," Matt replied. "Then your man went for his gun and I shot him."

"Alice," said McCandish, glancing down at his wife. "Go on inside."

"But, Tom — "

"Do as I say!" the rancher snapped. "And you, Jim; take Mike around back and get him down off that damn' horse."

McCandish waited until his wife

had gone into the house and Jim had disappeared around the corner, leading the skittish death-horse. At last Matt said, "Well, I'll be moving along. I'm sorry, Mr McCandish. I understand your foreman was more like one of the family to you. I took no pleasure from killing him, but he had it coming."

"This fight," McCandish said suddenly. "Mike started it, did he?"

Matt said, "He came looking to spark a girl who didn't care much for his intentions."

"He threw the first punch?" McCandish pursued.

Matt replied honestly. "I threw the first punch."

"And this girl," McCandish went on. "Was she *your* girl?"

"She was nobody's girl."

"But she was the same girl I saw ridin' with you this afternoon?"

"Yes."

"So Mike came a-callin' on your girl and you didn't much like the idea?"

Matt saw how he was making it sound. "There wasn't one person there who cared for the things he was suggesting."

"So you decided to pick a fight," McCandish rasped, "and you killed him. And I guess that made you a real big man with them Easterners, huh?"

"I killed your man before he killed me," Matt replied tautly. "Now I've fetched him home for you to bury. Goodnight, Mr McCandish."

"Son," said McCandish, "you ain't goin' *nowhere*."

He jacked a shell into the rifle.

Matt sat right where he was. He said, "Mr McCandish, it's been a hell of a night. Don't push me any further."

"It's just that I'm kind of curious. Mike was a good man. I never yet met the son he couldn't lick in a fight," said McCandish.

"You've met him now," Matt replied without arrogance.

"Get down offen that horse, Dury,"

McCandish barked sharply. "Let's see if you're as good with them fists as you say you are."

Matt sighed. "I'm not going to fight you, McCandish," he said. In truth, he didn't think he had another fight left in him tonight, for his muscles had started to cramp up, he could no longer feel his top lip and his knuckles felt raw.

"Climb down, I said," the rancher hissed through clenched teeth.

Matt worked up some spit and let it go in a line off to one side. "Go to hell."

He started to turn his pony around, but McCandish came a pace out towards him, pointed his long gun at the animal's forehooves and fired straight into the dirt.

The blast of the shot was tremendous in the night-time stillness. It scared hell out of Matt's pony, and with a panicky neigh it reared up to paw at the sky. It took Matt by surprise, too, unseated him and plunged him to the ground with a crash that knocked the wind out of him and stirred up fresh pain in his punished body.

The men over by the bunkhouse came forward a few steps, though it was not clear if they were thinking of joining in or intending to stop this thing before it went too far. Alice McCandish appeared back in the doorway, and Jim hustled back around front at a run.

Matt rolled up onto his knees just as McCandish tossed the rifle aside and came to tower above him, his big, scarred hands folding into deadly weapons. "Come on, then, Dury," he said. "You're so damned clever with your fists. Shuck them irons and see how you do against me."

Matt fought down a sudden blaze of temper. No. No . . . He couldn't afford to lose his head. That wasn't the way to handle this. But he knew he couldn't afford to get into another fight, either, not so soon after the last one, and not against so big a man. He must settle this quickly.

"I'm waitin', Dury . . . " said McCandish.

"Pa . . . "

"Stay out of this, Jim!"

Matt sensed McCandish looming above him. He got one foot under him and prepared to push erect. Instead he brought his right fist up between McCandish's legs and hammered him hard in the pellets. He heard Alice scream, heard Jim cry something hard to understand, but most of all he heard the rancher give out a high, half-choked wheeze of pain. Matt came up straight then, drew his right-side Tranter and brought it up and around in a short arc that slapped the rancher in the face and whipped his head sideways. The wheeze McCandish had voiced just seconds earlier turned abruptly into a bloody gurgle and he buckled like a concertina, one hand holding his groin, the other cupping his mouth in an effort to catch or hold in some blood and teeth.

Alice and Jim hurried to the fallen

man's aid. Watching them, Matt felt sick. He'd had no wish to fight dirty. But he'd had little choice. And in any case, there was no time for regrets now. The deed was done.

He turned and held the onlookers transfixed with the gun in his fist. "Listen up," he said. "I don't want any more trouble. Jim here saw exactly how your foreman met his end. It was his own double-dealing that killed him." He reached out with his free hand and grabbed his pony's trailing reins. "I'm leaving now. God help the man who figures to try and stop me."

One of the hired men held his hands up and said, "Go ahead an' welcome, mister." He glanced down at McCandish. "Mike Dean was no great loss, believe me."

Matt nodded through the darkness, then swung up into the saddle, looked down at McCandish, at McCandish's wife and son, gathered around him. "I'm sorry," he said, meaning it. "I really am."

The fallen rancher muttered something from out of his ruined mouth that sounded awful like *you bastard*.

Matt turned his horse and got out of there at a gallop.

★ ★ ★

He rode through the night, caught up with the last of the wagons sometime around one-thirty or so in the morning, glassy-eyed and aching but glad to be back among friends again. He made a brief pause beside the Minto wagon to assure Charlotte — and especially Rachel — that he had survived his unpleasant task unscathed, then made straight for the head of the column, and Sam.

Everyone there, animal and human, was dog-tired and footsore. But they had come a fair space, and Sam figured to spell the emigrants some time around dawn.

"How'd McCandish take it?" he asked after a time, careful to betray nothing of the relief he felt at having his boy back in one piece.

Matt sighed. "Pretty much how Jim figured he would."

"What happened?"

Matt told him. "Time I left, he was mad as a wet hen, and nobody could rightly blame him, after what I did to him. But he was like Dean. He brought it on himself."

"You think he might take it further?"

"Well, it'll be a while before he can fork a horse comfortably, and if the hired men I saw were anything to go by, there wasn't much love lost for Dean."

"That's somethin', I guess," Sam opined. "Still, I won't be sorry to leave this neck o' the woods. That McCandish, he struck me as a powerful hater."

"Maybe we'd ought to put out some riders to watch our back trail, then. Just to be on the safe side."

Sam bobbed his head. "I reckon. I'm startin' to get a little itchy 'bout this here Django Reilly, too. I figured he'd have made his move on us by now, if he was gonna make one at all."

"Maybe that's what he wants us to think."

"That's my reasonin'," Sam agreed. "That's why I think we'll go ahead an' arrange a little welcomin' committee for 'im, anyway."

They spelled the train at dawn, sent out pickets and allowed the exhausted emigrants to catch up on some of their postponed rest as the sky turned grey, then pink, then red, then amber and finally blue. Sam gave them till noon, then got them all moving again, and kept them trekking towards the north and west along the military road. He pushed them fiercely from here on, always following the silver strip of the North Platte River as the days melted into one another, and if the emigrants thought they'd known hardship under Galveston Jones, then Sam soon showed them exactly what hardship really was. The days warmed up. Dust and blowflies clogged the air. Axles screeched discordantly as the miles trundled slowly past beneath them.

Even when they finally reached civilisation, in the shape of Chimney Rock, Sam refused to let them tarry for any length of time. But they encountered no further trouble, from McCandish *or* Reilly.

He slowed the pace a little once they left Chimney Rock behind them, fearing some kind of rebellion if he continued to spur them on as he had. And the settlers' flagging spirits lifted a touch when they reached Scotts Bluff a little over two days and thirty-odd miles later. But even here he allowed them only one day for a hoot and a holler — as much of a hoot and a holler as any of these strait-laced greenhorns were capable of, anyway. Even so, it was a good peaceful time, which Sam elected to spend wisely — in the company of Jessica Berry.

There was some open, flat grassland

just outside the town and the settlers, under Sam's orders, had stalled their wagons there late the previous evening. Now, as the new day slowly matured, groups of men in buoyant humour tramped off to take a look around town. Some of the women also decided to explore the town, while others merely took the opportunity to wash out clothes and mind the children and catch up on some socialising without their menfolk getting in the way.

A vacation atmosphere had descended over the camp by the time Sam approached the preacher's wagon sometime around ten o'clock, having washed and shaved in cold water at first light and spent — at least to Matt, who had watched him secretly, and with some amusement — an inordinate amount of time combing his hair just right. Now Sam doffed his hat, nodded his good mornings and knelt to greet his fat Abyssinian cat, who, in the last couple of weeks, had adopted Jessica just as thoroughly as Jessica had adopted her.

"'Mornin', reverend. Miss Jessica."

Reverend Berry had been inspecting his oxen with one of the doctors, who was doubling as a veterinarian. Now he looked up, left the pill-roller to it and came over, all smiles. "Ah, good morning, Mr Judge. I thought you might have gone into town with some of the others."

"Actually, reverend, I thought I'd just step across an' ask Jessica here if she'd care to go for a ride this afternoon." Rather weakly he added, "Must get awful cramped, bein' stuck up on that there high seat like you are most days."

To his surprise, the priest's face lit up almost as much as that of his sister. "That is a capital notion, Mr Judge. We will be delighted to accompany you. Shall we say one o'clock?"

Sam had to fight hard to mask his irritation. We? *We?* How had the preacher come to include himself in the invitation? "Uh . . . sure," Sam replied. He caught Jessica's eye and was gratified to see that she obviously shared his disappointment that they would not be alone. But there was a long way to go yet before they reached Spruce Valley, he guessed. There'd be other times.

Sam might have relented a little as wagon-captain, but it was *only* a little. By four o'clock the following morning the camp was a hive of activity. By seven the train was once again stretched out into a mile-long, canvas-covered snake, and soon Scotts Bluff was just a memory.

The land closed in a bit over the next couple of days, as the prairie rose and dipped into more broken, timber-studded country. Once, they saw some riders about half a mile further south, hazing a sizeable herd of cattle southeast. Later that same afternoon Sam spied a shepherd working his flock of sheep towards the markets in the east. But other than these signs of life, the land appeared to be empty and isolated.

They reached Fort Laramie about half a week later, and again Sam allowed his train of emigrants to enjoy a day's respite from the usual backbreaking business of travel. Fort Laramie was an adobe-walled army barracks and trading-post, and the stopover offered the settlers a chance to swap gab with off-duty soldiers and rub shoulders with pacified Sioux.

A day later they were back on the move. By Sam's reckoning, they would keep to the military road for another sixty, seventy miles, then leave the trail, cross the river and head through Arapaho country and up into the mountains, where lay this earthly paradise, Spruce Valley.

But a day out of Fort Laramie, they ran into Django Reilly.

It came about like this.

The land had already started breaking up, and the trail ahead began to snake back and forth until about a quarter of a mile distant it followed something of a gully between two timbered downgrades and finally disappeared from sight around a curve. Having his suspicions about such a potentially ideal ambush-spot, Sam brought up his right hand to signal a halt, then rode ahead to check it out. The gully, so it transpired, only ran for about half a mile, if that, then opened out onto the grassy flats again.

Reaching the far end, he sat Charlie there for a while, listening to the silence, running his mild grey eyes up and across one rise, then the other. His horse blew, impatient to get moving again. But Sam was intrigued by that silence. There were no bird-cries coming from these thick woods. And yet he felt sure there were birds roosting within its complex framework of interwoven branches.

Maybe someone else was in there with them, then.

The thought gave him an itchy feeling around the nape of the neck, but he knew better than to betray his misgivings. He just sat there a moment longer, then finally turned the roan and kicked it over into an easy canter back the way he'd come.

By the time he reached the stalled train, Matt was sitting his horse beside the first wagon in line, waiting for him, as was Reverend Berry, who was a-foot. As Sam hauled in before them, his young companion's expression asked the question.

Sam said, "We'll take it nice 'n' easy through yonder channel, and I want at least a ten-yard gap between this here wagon an' the next one in line. Reverend; first sign o' trouble, you an' your people get your heads down an' don't put 'em up again till the smoke clears, you hear me?"

Reverend Berry gulped. "You really think this might be a trap, then?"

"I think it's good *spot* for a trap," Sam replied.

He watched the preacher trot back down the line as he loosened his .44 in its holster.

Word was passed back down the

201

line. After a while, Sam turned Charlie back to the northwest and spurred out ahead with Matt right beside him. The first wagon in line jerked into motion and very shortly after that, the next schooner down followed slowly in its wake.

The procession entered the gully cautiously. The entire train seemed to be holding its breath, adding to the preternatural hush which had descended over the ancient watercourse.

Now the only sounds were those of the high-stepping horses, the creak and scrape of the first wagon and the heavy snorting and grunting of the big-eyed oxen in the traces. Sam rode with his guts wound tight. But foot after foot they went deeper into the gully, yard after yard, and nothing happened. Maybe he was wrong about this. Maybe. But it wasn't often he was in error over such deadly matters.

They made it about halfway down the gully. Sam scoured the leafy shadows on the left, Matt the right. Nothing moved up in there, nothing that they could see, at least, save wind-ruffled scrub.

Three-quarters of the way along the gully.

Still nothing.

The trail curved a bit ahead of them. After that the downgrades began to ease off and melt into the flats beyond. Sam walked his roan around the curve with Matt beside him and the first wagon swaying along behind them.

And that's when they saw them.

Not that you could very well miss them, for the line of men and horses was strung right across the trail ahead of them, each man there unmistakably a hardcase loaded for bear, willing to fight and kill to take whatever he could from whoever he could.

Sam caught his breath in his throat and then let it out slowly. So . . . he *had* been right, then. After all these weeks and all these miles, he and Matt were finally going to get the chance to mix it up with Django Reilly.

And there was certainly no mistaking

that sonofabitch, for he was sitting astride a fine-limbed palomino stud at the approximate centre, and a little ahead, of the dozen-strong line of men flanking him, wide-shouldered, thin-hipped, long in the leg and unshaven. A black, flat-brimmed Stetson threw grey shadow down across a long, swarthy face that was aged far beyond its twenty eight years. He had thick black hair and keen brown eyes. His mouth was wide, with an easy, arrogant set to it. He wore a sweat-stained blue flannel shirt and canvas cotton pants tucked into fancy-stitched boots. Around his waist were buckled two gunbelts. In the left pocket he carried a long-barrelled .44. In the right sat a silvered .45. He favoured a big, sabre-handled Confederate Bowie knife in a fancy bead-decorated sheath, Sam noted, and he held a brand-new repeater casually across his lap. His skin had been ravaged by the pox at some stage of his life; now his hollow cheeks were mottled and pitted, but he had about him an air of supreme confidence and charisma. He was also without doubt a cold, pitiless bastard.

Just in back of Reilly sat another hard-looking son. He was older than Reilly by about a dozen years, heavier too, with either Mexican or Indian blood in him. His big features were set into a squarish kind of face, with a bushy black beard, yellow, evenly-spaced teeth and cool, very black eyes. He, like the rest of them, was dressed in hard-wearing jeans, fancy boots dripping with big-rowelled Mexican spurs. A sabre hung scabbarded at his left hip, counterpointing the butt-forward big Colt's Dragoon on his right. He also carried a rifle across the pommel of his fancy, silver-inlaid Mexican saddle.

Sam ran his eyes across face after face. Each one wore a cock-sure smirk. Taking whatever you fancied whenever the mood took you, inspiring fear in decent folks; it probably made them all feel real good. He thought about all the crimes these fellers were said to have committed, both here and down southwest, and made up his mind there and then to plug as many of them as he could.

He reined in when no more than about a dozen feet separated him from Reilly. Matt drew down a little off to his right. Behind them, the driver of the first wagon tooled his vehicle to a halt behind them and a little off to Sam's left.

Sam nodded a greeting. "It's Django Reilly, am I right?"

Surprise showed briefly in Reilly's eyes. Then his smile broadened and crinkled up the weathered skin around them. "You know who I am," he said, quite proud of his evident fame.

"Uh-huh."

"Then you know why I'm here?"

Sam nodded again. "You figure to rob us," he said.

Reilly appeared offended. "Not rob, *amigo*. Collect a toll."

Sam shrugged. "Whichever. Let's just get to it, shall we?"

Reilly said, "You have a name, my friend?"

"Judge."

"Well, you strike me as a man of the world, Judge. An' I sure want you to know that me an' my *compadres* here 'preciate you takin' such a sensible attitude to this. Las' feller we stopped along this stretch here, he wasn't half so reasonable. He put up a fight. An' do you know what?" Reilly assumed an expression of mock sorrow. "He died."

"Too bad," Sam commented. "Say, Reilly — you ain't got any cigars on you, I suppose?"

Reilly laughed. This was something new in his experience. This old man wasn't like the others. He knew who Reilly was, but he didn't seem to have the sense to show any fear or respect. Well, he'd learn his mistake before long. Reilly would teach him personally. Without turning around, he said, "Espada, give the man a cigar."

The big bearded *hombre* reached his left hand into his shirt pocket and pulled out a long, thin cheroot. He leaned forward with a creak of saddle-leather, put the smoke into Reilly's outstretched hand, and Reilly passed it over. "Here, my friend Judge."

Sam nudged Charlie closer and took the smoke, then plugged it into the corner of his mouth. "Obliged to you, Reilly," he said conversationally.

The halfbreed raised one eyebrow. "Espada, a light for the gentleman."

But Sam stopped him. "No. Thanks, anyway. I think I'll save it for afterwards."

"After we have collected out toll, yes?" Reilly asked.

"No," Sam replied. "After I've put pennies on your eyes."

He drew his Remington in that moment and shot the outlaw point-blank in the chest, and his bullet scrambled up Reilly's digestive system and tore him backwards out of his saddle with his shirt-front smouldering and a look of surprise fixed on his pock-marked face.

Not surprisingly, all hell broke loose. The palomino stud danced sideways, trampling its dead rider. Sam turned his Remington on the bearded feller, Espada, but Espada was already turning his horse around to bring his rifle up to line, and he missed. Matt drew his right-side Tranter and began to empty it into the confused line of would-be robbers, but their own prancing horses were making them difficult targets to hit.

The man on the high seat of the wagon reached down to scoop up a handgun which he then began to use to thin out their ranks — and from the back of the wagon poured a complement of eight of the best marksmen Reverend Berry had been able to round up — that welcoming committee Sam had talked about.

The element of surprise lasted for

all of ten seconds. Matt shot one of Reilly's men off his horse and when the sonuver jumped back up onto his feet and slammed his rifle-stock up to his shoulder, he let him have one more bullet, fairly chewing him up and spitting him out.

The men behind the wagon loosed off a withering volley. The gully walls trapped the sound and amplified it so that all the thunder was enough to bust a man's eardrums. Espada got off one shot, realised with a curse that long guns were impractical for up-close fighting like this, and turned his mount to get out of there.

Another saddle emptied. A horse screamed and went down heavily, punching dust up around its dead frame. Another mount stumbled across it, regained balance, but not before it threw its rider over its head.

Lead ripped holes in the canvas of the wagon and gouged splinters from its sideboards. One of the settlers screamed and twisted sideways to land in a red heap. Sam saw one of Reilly's men hip around in the saddle of his retreating mount and throw another shot back at them. Holding Charlie down to a sissy kind of dance, he thumbed back the hammer, tracked the varmint, squeezed the trigger and removed a fist-sized chunk of his spine.

It was over then, the first round anyway. Reilly's men were out of there, following Espada's lead.

Sam turned the old roan sideways-on and yelled for the men over by the wagon to cease fire. Both he and Matt reloaded their handguns as fast as they could. Then Sam threw a glance at Matt, and when Matt nodded he bawled, *"All right — let's ride!"*

As one, they kicked their animals into pursuit. They'd accounted for five of the robbers, including Reilly himself. But that still left eight of the bastards. Eight sore losers who might figure to come back some time soon and have their revenge.

A black man in a grey shirt and

shotgun chaps had elected to send his gelding up the slope towards the cover of the timber. Matt shot him in the shoulder. He fell forward over his horse's thick, glistening neck, turned the creature and with a yell of defiance, returned fire. Matt shot at him again; missed; once more; didn't.

Once out beyond the confines of the gully, Espada and the others gave their animals free rein. A couple of stragglers twisted around to shoot at their pursuers. Lead whined around the Texans like blowflies. Sam tried to block the sound of it out of his mind and concentrate on returning fire. He shot one man, watched him back-somersault out of his rig and thud face-first into the grass, then plugged the second with a chest-wound from which recovery was nigh-on impossible.

Then it really *was* over, and he shortened Charlie's rein. With some regret, the old horse slowed to a halt. Moments later Matt joined him, and as they emptied their hot revolvers once again, each man breathing hard and smudged by combat, they watched Espada and the four survivors skin out across the wide prairie like Old Nick himself was on their trail.

8

SOMEWHERE in all the confusion Sam had lost his recently-acquired cigar. He'd also taken a bullet-crease in the left biceps, a fact of which he had been entirely unaware until the heat of battle wore off and he realised that his arm was stinging like a bitch and his shirt-sleeve was wet and red.

He could have used that cigar about then.

They walked their horses back to the wagon train and discovered that two of the marksmen had picked up superficial wounds in the fray, but apart from that, the only fatalities had been on Reilly's side.

As Sam dismounted, Jessica Berry shouldered through the crowd of still-nervy settlers who'd come ahead to inspect the carnage up close. When she saw the bloodstain on his upper arm her hand went to her mouth and she hurried across to him and urged him by frantic gestures to sit down. Then she tore the sleeve open and inspected the damage.

Everyone had a question on his lips. And everyone expected Sam to have an answer for it. He didn't, so he ignored them. Matt saw Rachel Minto there in the forefront of the crowd and went on over to see her.

Jessica finished her hurried examination of Sam's wound. Once she realised that it looked far worse than it actually was, some of the urgency went out of her. Reverend Barry hovered nervously in the background, watching as one of the doctors came and patched him up. Then Sam went in search of his spare shirt, stripped down to the waist and threw the ruined one aside.

He felt tired and jumpy, just like he always did in the hour or so after violence. But the breeze helped to cool the fire in his arm, and the trees along both ridges had come alive with birdsong once again. "We'll camp in the swale just the other side of this timber, reverend," he decided at length, struggling to button his shirt one-handed. Jessica hurried forward to help him, and he found her ministrations most pleasing. "I doubt them other fellers'll come back again right away, if at all, but you'd better make arrangements to double the guard tonight to be on the safe side."

Berry nodded. "I'll attend to it at once. I'll see to it that the deceased receive a decent burial while I'm about it."

"I can save you some trouble there, reverend," Sam replied, not liking what was about to follow but knowing as he always had that it had to come out sooner or later. "Them there robbers got to be taken back to Fort Laramie. Matt's already gone to find a couple men to help him get 'em there."

"Ah, of course. I was forgetting. The authorities must be informed. And however mean they were in life, the

216

dead should receive proper burial, in hallowed ground."

"I was thinkin' more about the reward money that's waitin' to be collected," Sam told him, saying it quickly to get it over and done with.

The preacher's lip curled as he digested that. Jessica stopped buttoning his shirt and looked up at him with a strange expression in her dark eyes, like she was seeing him for the first time. After a spell Berry said, "The reward money, Mr Judge? *Blood* money, you mean?"

Sam was about to reply when the softest sound drew his attention, and he turned. Charlotte Minto was heading towards them, some of her earlier enmity towards him now forgotten.

Aw, shoot, he thought. *She's all I need right now*.

The handsome redhead came to a halt and regarded him with a smile. "Ah, Mr Judge. I just thought I would come over to make sure you were all right."

"I'm fine, ma'am, thank you for your concern."

The woman threw a disparaging glance at Jessica. "Not that I imagined for one moment that you would lack for comfort," she remarked. Then she picked up something in their expressions that made her frown. "I'm sorry, reverend. Am I interrupting something?"

Berry dipped his head. "I am afraid you are, Mrs Minto. Something rather . . . distasteful."

Charlotte looked from one of them to the other, awaiting further explanation. When no such explanation materialised, she said, "Whatever do you mean, reverend?"

Before Berry could respond, Sam cut in. "It's pretty straightforward, ma'am, though I don't anticipate that you'll find it much to your likin'." And he repeated to her pretty much what he'd already said to the Berrys.

He was right; she didn't like it, not one bit. But at least she heard him out. At last she spoke. She was a bold one, Sam thought, and her very bluntness must have distanced her from the more genteel women of New York or Pennsylvania or wherever in hell she'd come from.

"Is that how you make your living, then, Mr Judge?" she asked. "By hunting bounty?"

"No, ma'am."

"And yet you are quite willing to claim the reward on those dead men."

"Uh-huh."

The woman turned to Berry. "And what is your objection, reverend?"

The preacher was beside himself. "With respect, Mrs Minto, I should have thought that was obvious! To kill a man in self-defence is one thing, but to kill him and then take *money* for the deed — "

"If I kill a man," Sam spat irritably, "you can be damn' sure there's a good reason for it, reverend. An' you can be damn' sure the sonofabuck in question deserves all he's got comin' to him. An'

219

if I catch or kill a feller with a price on his head — to defend *you* people, I might add — I'd be a fool not to claim it."

To his surprise, Mrs Minto nodded. "That is quite right, Mr Judge. Reverend, I think perhaps you should consider the greater good here. The brave men who helped in the defence of the train just now *should* receive a reward. And you know as well as I that, as self-reliant as we may be in Spruce Valley, there will be times when we shall require money in order to conduct commerce with the outside world."

"Ma'am?" Sam asked, thoroughly bewildered.

"How much is the reward upon the dead men?" Charlotte enquired bluntly.

Sam did some swift mental acrobatics. Until this moment, he hadn't really thought to make a tally. At last he said, "Nineteen hundred dollars. That's five hundred dollars for Reilly an' two hundred apiece for each of his associates."

"Then we shall take thirty-five percent to replenish our funds," Charlotte decided.

"Thirty-five percent — !" Now it was Sam's turn to be beside himself. "But that's better'n six hundred dollars!"

"I do hope you will not insult us by insisting that we take any more," the redhead said with a malicious glint in her eyes.

"Mrs Minto . . . " began Reverend Berry.

Sam clenched his teeth. All the cuss-words of four different languages ran swiftly through his mind. The woman had him over a barrel. And hell, it was true enough that some of the men *had* helped him and Matt rout Reilly's bravos, he guessed.

"All right," he said begrudgingly. "You got a deal." A cat-with-the-cream smile appeared on Charlotte's mouth. Even Reverend Berry seemed to accept the compromise. But Jessica gave Sam a glance loaded with disappointment, then turned and hurried away, and he realised in that moment that he would have given the whole nineteen hundred dollars not to have disillusioned her so.

Lord, how he craved that cigar!

★ ★ ★

Matt and three men rode out in the late afternoon, trailing behind them a bizarre column of blanket-wrapped bodies bellydown across their horses.

"This is all gonna take some time," the younger Texan had said earlier. "We can likely make Fort Laramie by mid-day tomorrow, but we'll probably have to hang around a while until someone somewhere decides to authorise payment of the reward."

"Well, it'll take as long as it takes, I guess," Sam replied with a sigh. "But I'd as soon press on as wait for you here. On the move we'll make a harder target."

"Keep moving then, and we'll catch you up."

Matt studied their maps before leaving, to get an approximate idea of the route they would have to follow on the way back. Then, as the sun began its westward slither, Sam watched his lean companion swing aboard his hull, tip his hat to Rachel Minto and then lead his grisly cavalcade out and away to the southeast.

The night passed without event. Sam's arm throbbed like hell. Every time he happened to catch sight of Jessica Berry on the far side of the camp, she was very careful to avoid his gaze and busy herself with other matters.

Well, he should have let that be a lesson to him. Get yourself involved with a woman and sooner or later she'll turn on that disapproving look and try to change you. At least that's what he told himself as he rolled into his blanket that night. But he couldn't help feeling guilty. He knew he had let her down, perhaps let *himself* down too. But what did she think he was — a knight in shining armour? Well, he wasn't. He was just a man. And she knew that now.

Out ahead, the sawtooth blue mountains loomed high and thickly-forested, with snow still clinging stubbornly to the highest peaks. The prairie stretched away on all sides, flat and emerald-green as far as the eye could see, and the grass grew thick and tall as a horse's belly. Occasionally there were trees, and sometimes there were dips and swells to be negotiated, but for the most part the travelling was straightforward and without problem.

They had some bad luck when the time came to leave the Oregon Trail, assume a more northerly course, cross the North Platte and begin their ascent into the high country. Two wagons capsized halfway through the river crossing and in the ensuing confusion two men drowned. It was a sobering time and it had a discouraging influence upon the emigrants, more so because the river crossing was the last major obstacle before they began the final run up to Spruce Valley.

Sam pushed them hard as a consequence, to stop them from thinking too much about the frailty of life and the constant presence of death in these wild, wide-open spaces. A day later they left the rushing river behind them and began to ford still more endlessly-rippling grassland.

This was Arapaho country, but if there were any Arapaho out there watching them, then they were either well-hidden or downright invisible. Jessica Berry continued to keep her distance from him, but that just gave Sam one more reason for pushing the settlers so hard — to stop himself from thinking too much about the preacher's silent sister.

At last the land began to rise beneath man and beast and iron tyre. Weathered pines clustered to form large bosques. Aspen shoved up from out of tangles of wild flowers. The land rose higher and steeper. The going became slower and more cautious. Soon the white-capped peaks looked close enough to reach out and grab.

The air thinned out. Exhaustion seemed to come that much sooner. They were in or near the Wind River country now, where game was plentiful, the scenery was breathtaking and a feller could really believe he was the last man on earth.

Matt and the three men he'd taken with him caught up with them in a wide, tree-fringed bowl about a week and a half later, and after all the usual greetings had been exchanged and everyone had caught up on their newsmongering, there followed a division of the spoils, so to speak. The settlers received $665, which Reverend Berry took with some distaste and locked away in a strong-box in back of his wagon. But that still left Sam and Matt with better than twelve hundred dollars. Even allowing for the settlers' cut, it was by no means a bounty to be sneezed at.

The return of the men went some of the way towards assuaging the grief many of the settlers still felt about the death of two of their number, but Sam still kept them on the move, for it was only a matter of time before they reached their destination. There was something in Matt's manner that put him on his guard, though, and as the two of them rode out ahead of the column, he turned a little in the saddle to find out exactly what it was.

Matt was not in the least bit surprised that the older man had divined that something was wrong. "Could be something," he said, scanning the country around them, "or it could be nothing."

"Well, let's hear it, anyway."

Matt put his thoughts into order. "There wasn't much to do around Fort Laramie while we was waiting for the authorities to approve our claim for the reward money, 'cept hang around the trading-post and drink flat beer. But our third night there, things got a little more interesting."

"Oh?"

"Yeah. Feller name of Brandon came up and offered me a job. Seems, he's a fixer from someplace down around the Nebraska-Kansas line, and he was trying to put together a crew to go raise hell among a bunch of settler-folk trending up into these here mountains."

Sam narrowed his gaze. "Us?" he said.

"Couldn't hardly be anyone else."

"What did you tell 'im?"

"That I already had a job. But the pay was real respectable, and though he wouldn't say who it was he was working for, I suspicion that's kind of obvious, too."

Sam nodded. "McCandish," he said quietly. "Damn him. I told you he was a powerful hater, didn't I?"

"Well, this feller Brandon, he let on that he wasn't finding it all that easy to recruit much talent in these parts, so maybe nothing much'll come of it. But maybe it'd pay you to sleep with one eye open for a while."

Sam's focus sharpened. "*Me?*"

Matt nodded. "I figure to ride on back and see McCandish about it personally."

Sam considered that. "Now hold on a minute, Matt. Could be that's exactly what McCandish wants."

"I don't doubt for one moment that it is. He's likely only figuring to have a crack at these Easterners to get at me."

"We'll *both* go settle with him," Sam decided. "We'll get these here folks settled into Spruce Valley an' then we'll ride on back a-ways an' have it out with him once an' for all." He paused. "Meantime, we'll keep this to ourselves."

Matt agreed, then frowned. "Oh, yeah. Almost forgot." He reached back into his right-side saddlebag. "Picked you up a little something while I was at Fort Laramie." And he handed over a clutch of cigars.

Sam's eyes lit up. "Hell, I *knowed* there was a reason I kept you around, son. Obliged."

They made camp early and spent most of the next day trekking ever deeper into the high wilderness, and along towards the end of the afternoon, Sam called a halt and rode on ahead by himself and disappeared through a stand of aspen about half a mile away.

Behind him, the men and women and children of the Spruce Valley wagon train waited in silence, worn down by thousands of miles of travel and hardship and hoping against hope that all of that was about to end very, very soon.

Matt spurred his pony up the line, hauling down when he came to the Minto wagon. The women acknowledged him with a nod, but nothing more. He saw the expectation in their faces and sensed it in their obvious distraction. Butterflies and bumble bees cut through the warm air. Oxen snorted and steamed. Horses sidestepped impatiently. A milk-cow swished her tail at the flies gathering along her back, and the bell around her neck tinkled softly.

Minutes passed. Then there was a movement up ahead. Sam came out of the trees at a steady canter. They watched him come back across the wide green swale and rein in alongside the preacher's schooner. He leaned forward and said something that no-one else could hear. Reverend Berry nodded and hopped down from the wagon-seat to come back along the line, squinting myopically in the bright sunlight.

All eyes fixed upon him as he raised both palms toward the sky. "We shall give thanks!" he yelled. "Pass the word back along the line, if you will; Spruce Valley lies just the other side of that timber. We have reached our destination, my brothers and sisters!

We have come home at last!"

A great cheer rose up. Men threw their hats high into the air. Women hugged each other and wept. There was some praying as a general feeling of euphoria settled upon them, but then came impatience, for the settlers were anxious to travel that last half-mile or so, to trundle through the grey-green gloom of the woods and finally enter Spruce Valley, and confirm for themselves that all the adversity had been worthwhile.

* * *

It was.

It was worth all of that and more.

It was, in fact, just about everything that Reverend Berry had said it would be.

It was a grass-rich meadowland that ran northwesterly for some ten or twelve miles and stretched three miles from one timbered rim to the other. A stream meandered across the valley floor. They saw white spray dancing over smooth stones and lichen-covered rocks. Later they found out that it came from a mirror-still lake far beyond the northernmost timber.

As they began their descent into the wooden haven, protected from the elements — and the rest of the world — by ramparts of spruce and fir and pine, they spied a herd of mule deer drinking at the stream's edge. The animals turned their heads and watched them from out of curious, sloe eyes as they came down the rough, natural trail of shale and buffalo grass and pine needles. Then, spooked, they darted away suddenly and vanished into the trees. Down along the stream-banks, other tracks proliferated; mostly bear, coyote and elk.

The wagons came down into the pristine beauty of it all, russet-coloured in the approaching sunset, with men pointing here and there and their wives nodding in understanding, acceptance or agreement, and their children all keyed-up by the excitement of the moment.

They were, as the preacher had said, coming home. At last.

Over the next week or so the valley became a hive of activity as men drove in stakes to mark out the positions of their cabins and others stamped off into the hills to cut timber. Soon the high-country air was filled with the sounds of chopping and the ominous creak and tear of weakened wood as tree after tree crashed to earth. Wagons went up there empty and came back piled high with logs. Up on the southernmost ridges, looking down on it all, it was easy to see that the community was beginning to take shape. The commercial section was going to be built at the centre of the metropolis, with the adzed-log cabins of the settlers surrounding it. Some of the men were already constructing a modest bridge to span the stream.

The emigrants appeared to thrive on toil. They started early and finished late. Their cooperative spirit blossomed.

It reaffirmed some of Sam's faith in human nature, although he wondered how long it would last. At the moment these Easterners had a common purpose. But what would happen once their community here was completed and each of them was free to pursue his own individual interest?

Some bright spark suggested they hold a celebration party at the end of the second week, which Sam and Matt should attend as guests of honour. In no time at all the proposal was seconded, and while the men continued about the business of construction, the women began to prepare the food. Some of Reverend Berry's enthusiasm for the festivities was dampened, however, when Sam took him aside one fine morning and told him that their little celebration would also have to serve as a farewell party.

The little pastor peered up at him, genuine sorrow on his face. "Do you *have* to leave, Mr Judge? I had started to entertain hopes that you might decide to stay with us."

"We only signed on to get you where you was goin', reverend," Sam reminded him. "An' Matt an' me, we just ain't the settlin' kind. I did it one time an' it pretty near finished me off."

Berry swallowed. "Well, I . . . I think I speak for everyone when I say we shall miss you both." He stuck out his hand and Sam shook with him.

Matt and Rachel spent much of their time exploring the valley together, but there was a kind of emptiness to their relationship now, as if they had both come to realise and finally accept that they were just killing time, until each went his or her separate way.

Log-piles sprang up everywhere. Carpenters hammered from dawn till dusk, imitating the woodpeckers so numerous in the surrounding forests. As much as Sam hated to admit it, the dedication of these greenhorns was inspiring. As the second week wore along, the cabins began to take on more form. Animals watched this human invasion inquisitively and with some unease. But if the settlers had any sense, they would try to live in harmony with the rest of nature, and not attempt to bend it to their will.

At last the day of the celebration party dawned. The women-folk spent most of their time filling trestle-tables with all manner of food, while the men strung home-made bunting across what would one day be their main street.

The celebration itself got underway some time around six o'clock that evening, and after Reverend Berry climbed up onto a makeshift podium and delivered a short but heartfelt speech acknowledging the debt they all owed to Messrs Judge and Dury for bringing them so far, and with so few casualties, the gathered settlers struck up an enthusiastic chorus of 'For They Are Jolly Good Fellows'. Then the men from Texas had their hands pumped by just about everyone there until, after a time, Sam managed to escape from all the well-wishers in order to go search for Jessica Berry.

She was not taking part in the festivities. He found her sitting in an old rocking chair on the far side of the wagon she shared with her brother, deep in thought. Mitzi was curled in her lap, and for a while Sam watched the woman stroking the cat's head, feeling a mixture of emotions. Finally he cleared his throat, disturbing her from her reverie, and came over. It was quieter away from the centre of all the merry-making, and those sounds that did carry this far seemed to have no business there, for tonight this was evidently a place of solitude and introspection.

"'Evenin', Miss Jessica," he said with a nod. Mitzi got up and hopped down to the ground, circled Sam's legs a couple of times and then slunk away into the gathering darkness.

Jessica made to rise, but Sam gestured that she should remain seated. He came closer, knelt beside her, reached out and took one of her hands in both of his. She made no attempt to pull away from him.

"Matt an' me'll be leavin' tomorrow," he said quietly. "Before we go, I jus' wanted to tell you how much I 'preciated your company on the trip, an' apologise for anythin' I did that might've offended you."

She reached out and put a finger on his lips to silence him. Then she glanced around and indicated their surroundings with her hands and asked her question with a shrug. She was trying to ask him why he didn't intend to stay and he told her. "Because that's the way I am, I guess. Always got to find out what's on the other side of the mountain. An' ol' Matt, he's just the same." He thought it best not to mention Tom McCandish, or what Matt had heard back in Fort Laramie, and what he and Matt intended to do about it.

She nodded soberly and turned her face away from him. He reached out, cupped her chin and gently eased her back around. She was crying, as he had known she would be. "I won't ever forget you, Jess," he told her honestly.

She pointed to her heart, then to him.

"Me you, too," he said swallowing.

He stiffened then, and she looked up at him in alarm. Her face asked the question, and he answered it as he rose to his feet. "I don't know. Thought I heard a sound . . . a gunshot."

She rose to stand beside him. They stood listening for a time, and peering out into the darkness, but all they could hear were the sounds of the revellers a hundred yards away.

"Must've been mistaken," he said after a spell.

He sensed the nearness of her and felt his determination wavering. She was everything he could possibly want in a woman. But he knew he couldn't stay here forever. Sooner or later the time would come when he'd just have to move on, or go crazy. It was as well to get it over and done with now, in order to avoid going through the whole sorry business again at some later stage.

He looked down at her. He wondered if he would ever again experience the sense of complete tranquillity she exerted over him. He didn't think so.

"I better go now," he said.

Before he could do any such thing, though, a cry tore through the cool evening air, and he spun around with his right hand swooping toward the butt of his .44.

"*Hey, look! They's a rider comin' in!*"

9

SAM headed back towards the main body of settlers at a sprint, vaguely aware that the preacher's sister had lifted her long skirt slightly above her ankles in order to hustle right along after him. When he reached the assembled roisterers, they were muttering uneasily among themselves. Slowing down, he called out, "All right, all right — what's goin' on here?"

Someone in the crowd turned and called back, "They's a rider comin', Mr Judge!"

He already knew that. But hearing it again now, he felt a ball of ice settle in his stomach. What could possibly have brought anyone out to this remote spot except trouble?

He wondered grimly if this was how the trouble with McCandish was going to begin.

He pushed through the crowd. The settlers saw him coming with his long-barrelled gun in his fist and wisely got out of his way. Matt fell into step beside him just as they made it through to the far side and came to a halt beside Reverend Berry and a few of the gutsier emigrants who had gone out a little ahead to keep track on the newcomer's approach. It was so quiet now that you could hear the throb of the horse's hooves growing ever louder in the twilit stillness.

Out ahead, cabin after cabin stood in various stages of completion. Piled logs lay everywhere. Wagons had been parked wherever their owners had decided to build their homes. The camp was caught up in the confusion of construction, but already a half-way organised layout could be seen emerging, and it was along what would eventually become the community's main thoroughfare that the lone rider was spurring his lathered horse.

He was coming on at break-neck

speed, and he was leaning forward loosely over his mount's pumping neck, evidently holding himself in the saddle with a titanic effort of will.

Sam cursed under his breath. It was trouble for sure, then. Question now was — what *kind* of trouble?

About forty yards out, the man's dark mustang broke stride a bit and came to a heaving, crabby kind of halt. The rider fell out of the saddle, unconscious or worse, and rolled onto his back with his arms stretched out to either side of him. His horse stood over him, head drooping, flanks lathered, lungs working like bellows.

There was just the slightest pause then. A moment later, the men from Texas went ahead at a cautious trot, guns in hand, eyes everywhere. They reached the fallen man and Matt knelt beside him. Although the cleared area chosen for the party had been well-lit by torches and cook-fires, the light out here was weak. Even so, there was no mistaking the identity of the newcomer.

Matt looked up over one shoulder and said, "It's Tom McCandish."

Sam knelt beside his partner as Matt reached a hand under the big rancher's head and cradled it. McCandish looked ghastly in the darkness. His skin was as white as paper and his eyes were screwed shut, as if he were in the middle of a nightmare and trying hard to wake up. There was blood on his shirt-front. It looked like tar through the shadows.

Sam stood up and called back for one of the doctors. The tall, angular feller with the brown leather case full of rattling surgical irons was already on his way out to them.

McCandish opened his eyes and said, "Uh . . . "

"Easy, McCandish," Matt said softly.

McCandish recognised his voice, turned his eyes only so that he could see Matt better, and a sick, fleeting grimace crossed his face. "Dury," he said breathlessly. "Hell . . . you're what this was all about . . . "

"What all *what* was about?" Sam asked, kneeling down again.

Somewhere down the line, McCandish had lost his hat. Now his once-florid complexion appeared to be the same colour as the cropped snowy hair around his bald head. He worked his lips for a while but no sounds came. His expression was one of desperation, urgency, determination. He coughed. The sound came out wet and bubbly. The doctor arrived, surgical irons rattling, and tried to shoo Sam and Matt out of the way, but McCandish stopped him.

"Hold up a minute, mister," he husked. "I got to speak first."

"Make it quick," the doctor said, kneeling, taking out a scalpel and cutting open the rancher's bloody shirt to get a better look at the wound.

"Someone shot you," Sam said flatly, to get started.

"They're up there," McCandish replied, raising his right hand to indicate the dark, timbered ridges to the south and east. "Five of them. I . . . I hired them. Figured to come up here after you . . . folks and teach Dury here a lesson."

"We guessed that," Sam said.

Surprise flashed in McCandish's hard eyes. "Figured to come up here . . . take Dury and . . . give him back some of the medicine he gave me. But them other fellers . . . " He shook his head, winced a little as the doctor pushed and prodded with exploratory fingers. "I didn't know it, but them other fellers . . . they meant to do you harm, the lot of you."

Sam's face tightened gravely. "One of 'em a big feller?" he asked. "Bearded, part Mexican? Favours a sabre on his left hip?"

McCandish nodded. "Calls hisself Espada," he said.

It was plain enough to guess what had happened, then. McCandish's fixer had unwittingly hired the survivors of Django Reilly's gang for him.

"I got no quarrel with any of you

other folks," McCandish said in a rasping, pain-clogged voice. "But them others . . . turns out they're fixing to get back at you for whatever it was you did to them."

The doctor yelled back down the way, "Someone fetch me some light here!"

"I . . . I told 'em to hell with that," McCandish went on. "They take my p-pay, they take my orders. But . . . there was an argument . . . they shot me . . . b-bastards . . . Didn't know what else to do, just rammed my spurs and came in to w-warn you . . . "

"All right," said Matt. "You've warned us, McCandish. Rest easy now."

The rancher closed his eyes. Unconsciousness seemed to wash over him like a tide.

"I'm going to have to operate on this man at once," the doctor announced without looking up.

Some of the settlers arrived carrying

lanterns. The doctor got to his feet, told them to forget his request for light and take the wounded man — gently, for God's sake — to his wagon. The Texans watched them lift McCandish up with some difficulty, for he was a big man, and carry him off.

Sam scanned the dark slopes. "If what McCandish said is true," he said pensively, "we got to get the rest of these folks under cover, fast."

Matt agreed. "Best get started right away, then."

They turned and started back towards the watching crowd. They got about a dozen feet before a man yelled something and pointed, and a woman beside him loosed off a shrill scream.

The men from Texas turned to face their back-trail once again. Immediately their attention was captured by five fireflies dancing through the darkness.

Fireflies?

Fireflies *hell*!

They heard hoofbeats then, coming in fast. Seconds later they distinguished the shapes of five horsemen thundering down on them, yelling at the tops of their lungs, each one waving a burning torch in his free hand.

Sam turned and bellowed, *"Find some cover, you people — quick, now!"*

As the settlers scattered and the air came alive with commotion and disorder, he wheeled back around, his Remington fairly leaping into his hand.

Espada was in the lead. He saw the sonuver's sabre clattering and banging against his hip as he urged his big horse down on them with yells and curses and jamming spurs.

Sam and Matt threw themselves aside and found cover fast. At the last moment, Espada tossed his burning torch into the first pile of logs he came to. He went past in a blur of motion and the Texans came out after him with their weapons blazing.

Their bullets missed.

Now the rest of Reilly's bravos

were crashing down the rough-and-ready main street, hurling their own flaming torches at any likely-looking target.

The bastards, Sam thought. *The cunning, callous bastards*. They were going to torch this entire valley if they could, and use the light of the fires to help them pick off these settlers.

He tracked one of the riders and fired another round. That also missed. He swore imaginatively. Handguns were no good at this range. He needed his carbine out here.

Already the flames of five separate fires were taking hold and multiplying. Here the front wall of a partially-built cabin was rapidly becoming an inferno. There the linseed-coated canvas-twill cover of a big wagon was erupting into flame. The horsemen thundered by and Sam fired one more shot. He struck lucky that time. One of the riders lurched forward in his saddle, somehow clung on, kept going, ploughing on through wildly-scattering

251

emigrants. His horse leapt high to clear one of the laden trestle-tables and he left the saddle with a scream, crashed down among all the dishes and bowls with a tinkle and smash of breaking glass.

The table collapsed beneath him. He rolled and writhed with the pain of his shoulder-wound. One of the fleeing settlers grabbed up the man's fallen Starr and shot him again, blowing him from up here to down there.

Sam surged after the departing horsemen with Matt right beside him. Women were screaming. Children were bawling. Men were yelling out in panic to try and find out what had happened to their scattered kin. Sam saw a woman lying facedown in the churned grass, still and lifeless. A few yards away, a man was sprawled on his back, broken-necked and trampled by the outlaws' horses. There were some other bodies scattered a little further away, men, women, a child. He hoped like hell that Jessica wasn't among them.

He went off into the darkness and through a maze of stalled wagons in search of his gear. He heard the shifting around of the spooked livestock in the rope corrals nearby, the weeping and wailing, the roar and spit of omnivorous flames.

At last he located his saddle and gear, hauled his Spencer from its sheath. A fresh wave of screaming told him that Espada and the others were coming back.

Good.

'Far as Sam was concerned now, it was pay-back time.

Shadows capered and gambolled around the valley, thrown by the ever-spreading fires. He hustled back and around all the wagons, aware of terrified men and women crouching wherever the darkness could conceal them. He was sweating. The air was filled with the angry crackle and hiss of the hungry flames as they consumed wood and buckled metal. He heard the thunder of horses and spun to face the darkness to the northwest. Sure enough, Reilly's bravos were coming back in, guns replacing torches this time, and the cold-blooded, kill-crazy sonsofbitches were firing indiscriminately at any target.

Matt must've had the same idea about long guns. On the far side of the cleared area, he came around a pile of logs with his Winchester blazing and bucking in his fists. His bullets slammed into the chest of the first horse in the line-up and the poor beast went down with a snap of forelegs and ploughed into the dew-slick grass. Its rider was a shortish, squarely-built man with a week's growth of stubble on his sun-darkened face. He came out of the saddle on the run, fell, came up shooting wildly.

Sam was already there. He took aim with the Spencer and shot him in the head.

The man slammed back against the grass minus a face, all twitching arms and legs.

Three to go.

Lead whined around them. The clamour of the flames was drowned only by the pounding of hooves as the outlaws galloped past again. Matt fired into them, missed, kept working the action and firing again — another saddle emptied in a shower of blood and brain matter.

And then there were two.

The metallic stink of blood took Sam back to the battlefields of the late war. He watched Espada and the one remaining survivor of the Reilly gang hurtle on for maybe thirty yards. Given the choice, they'd likely have cut their losses and got out of there then. But they didn't have a choice any more. There was a wall of flame blocking their path now; they had no option but to twist their horses around and come on back.

Espada's mouth opened wide to yell some profanity or another. Then he and the other man kicked their animals into a flat-out gallop back towards

Sam and Matt, firing wildly, their blood up, the killing-rage upon them, thoughts of their own safety of no great importance any more, so long as they could inflict more death and suffering themselves.

Matt jacked a fresh .44/40 into his Winchester, threw the stock of the saddle-gun up to his smeared cheek, took aim, fired. The man alongside Espada, a thin, sallow-faced *hombre*, took the shot in his right shoulder and lurched backwards under the impact. His yell turned into a scream. Matt worked the action, shot him one more time, and the bastard went backwards and sideways out of the saddle, one foot caught in the stirrup.

His horse dragged him dead and bouncing back past them. That just left one of them. Espada.

Sam watched the big bearded half-blood bearing down on him. There were no words to describe his expression in that moment. He stood right in the path of the oncoming horse, fingers whitening around the carbine in his grip.

Espada came on like a runaway train.

At the last moment, Sam leapt aside, twisted around, brought the Spencer up and knocked the son right out of his saddle.

Espada flew backwards through the air, dropped his handgun and landed with enough force to kick the air out of him. He was a fighter, though, and he was up again almost at once. His wicked, cool, very black eyes flashed down to his fallen Dragoon, then up to Sam, who was advancing on him with a face that promised murder. He knew he couldn't reach the weapon in time. So his right hand swept across his body and his fist closed around the handle of his sabre.

The blade came up out of its sheath with a whisper of burnished steel, and with another defiant bellow, he threw himself at Sam.

Sam fell back to avoid the slashing

sword. Espada came in fast, crowding him so that the Spencer became as good as useless. Sam heard Matt yell his name but ignored him, just threw the carbine aside and grabbed for the arm wielding the sabre.

Espada was about three inches taller than Sam, and maybe forty or fifty pounds heavier. But Sam's fighting blood was up, and right at that moment there was nothing more important to him than wiping this sonofabitch bastard off the face of the earth.

A test of strength ensued. Teeth clenched. Faces turned beet-red. Then Sam got a hold on Espada's wrist and he yanked backwards, dragging a yell from the halfbreed. He had a choice, then — either drop the sabre or go over backwards with it. He went backwards and took Sam down with him.

But Sam landed on top of him, and while he tried to peg Espada's sword-arm against the grass with his left hand, he used the right to gouge at his opponent's eyes.

Espada thrust him off, came up and flung himself on top. They rolled over in a confusion of limbs. Firelight flashed off the sabre's wicked edge. Watching, Matt felt helpless. The two combatants were in such a wild, shifting tangle now that he dare not use the Winchester for fear of hitting the wrong man.

They broke apart then and each man leapt to his feet. Espada came in again with the sabre slashing in vivid silver arcs. Sam leapt back, logic replacing some of his foolish anger at last, and he hauled his Remington and shot Espada in the shoulder.

Blood splashed from the wound. Espada's scream was high and woman-like. He dropped the sabre from nerveless fingers and the weapon fell softly into the grass.

His eyes widened as Sam bore down on him, teeth gritted, nostrils flared; then, suddenly, he twisted away, made a crazy, desperate lunge for the pistol he'd dropped when Sam had first knocked him out of the saddle.

Sam was away ahead of him, though. Even as Espada was reaching down to snatch up the gun, he — Sam — was reaching down to scoop up the sabre, and by the time Espada was wheeling back around to face him with the Dragoon in his fist, Sam was already there, right upon him, driving the blade in through his stomach and out through his back.

Espada's mouth yanked wide. His eyes bulged with shock and surprise and pain. He looked hideous. He screamed again.

Sam backed away from him, leaving the sabre where it was, the killing urge in him gone now, instead feeling shocked and nauseated by his actions.

The light went out of Espada's black eyes and his legs went out from under him. He was boneless when he hit the grass.

He was dead.

Weakness caught up with Sam in a rush that left him feeling light-headed. He wanted to go off somewhere quiet and throw up until there was nothing left inside him, and then he wanted to go to sleep and forget all about grudges and revenge and death, the weaknesses of men.

But the roar of the flames came back in on him as he stuffed the Remington away. There was still work to be done. And Matt was already trying to get it organised.

His voice was as sharp as any bullet-crack in the stunned silence. "All right, come on! We need a bucket-brigade from the stream to up here! Kennedy, get it organised right away! Wilson, I want you to find out who needs medical attention. Reverend! Try to establish some kind of hospital area back there, will you? You there, Comaskey — take some men and check on the livestock! And Mrs Minto; I want all the women and children rounded up and quartered someplace safe!"

The settlers watched him through wide, scared, confused eyes. No-one

moved. Then Sam clapped his hands
loudly.

"Come on, now, get the lead out!"
he bawled.

At last the spell was broken.

They got the lead out.

★ ★ ★

Dawn.

The dawn that followed a long, long
night.

Exhausted and smudged grey by
smoke, Sam and Matt sat their horses
midway up the southeastern slope
and surveyed the damage through
red-rimmed eyes.

The once-green valley floor was
now blackened and charred and ugly-
looking. Here and there scorched
timber still popped and cracked and
glowed faintly orange in the shifting
breeze. The inky shells of burnt-out
wagons sent faint wisps of grey smoke
up into the watery early-morning air,
where it hung like lengths of twine

before the breeze scattered it in a pall across the sky.

It was a sad, pathetic, discouraging sight.

The acrid stench of smoke still clung in their nostrils, to their clothes, in their hair. It clogged their raw throats and stung their bloodshot eyes. But they were lucky. Four settlers had died either during the attack or in the hectic hours that followed it, and a further seven — three of them children — were still suffering from shock. The bullet had been removed from Tom McCandish's chest and the big rancher was now sleeping in one of the tents they had erected in what had come to be known as the hospital area. The doctor said that with the right care, and barring infection, he should eventually pull through.

Sam shook his head at the sorry sight below him. To think that these people had come all this way just to have this happen to them. Everything

263

they had worked for, everything they had built in these last couple of weeks, had been wiped out. Their dream had turned into a nightmare. They had the best excuse in the world now to throw in the towel.

But damned if the women weren't already sifting through the wreckage to see what they could salvage of their belongings, while the men were earmarking what timber they could still make use of, and gathering in groups to point and talk about how best they could rebuild this or that.

"Riders," said Matt.

Sam turned his attention to the small group coming up the slope towards them. Reverend Berry and his sister, Charlotte Minto and her daughter. The Texans watched their approach in silence, and when the newcomers reined down, they nodded a tired greeting.

Reverend Berry regarded them from out of wire-framed spectacles that now played host to one cracked lens. "Good morning gentlemen," he said.

Sam nodded. "'Mornin', reverend — though I wouldn't necessarily say they was anythin' good about it."

To his surprise, Berry actually smiled, albeit briefly and kind of melancholy. "No matter how bad a situation may be, Mr Judge, it could always be *worse*." He glanced sideways at his companions, then said, "You are still leaving us today?"

Sam shrugged. "Got to get word to McCandish's wife an' son that he's all right. An' I run out of cigars again. Have to find me someplace to buy some more.

"Well," said the preacher, "God bless you both."

He reached over and they shook hands.

But Sam's attention was on Jessica, and Matt's was on Rachel. It was a moment heavy with emotion, charged mostly with regret and a certain reluctance to say goodbye. Jessica's trembling lips formed a painful smile as she and Sam looked at each other for the last time. Rachel reached up irritably to palm tears from her cheeks. Mitzi, now safely installed in Sam's right-side saddlebag, blinked her sea-green eyes sleepily.

Charlotte Minto said, "Tell me something, Mr Judge. And be honest with me, now."

"I'll try, ma'am."

"Do you remember that I once told you we Easterners might prove hardier than you gave us credit for?"

"I do indeed, ma'am."

She indicated the settlers milling around industriously below, ant-size from this distance. "Would you say I was right?"

He nodded. "An' then some, Mrs Minto. An' then some."

They stayed there for a short time, awkward in their farewells, and then the settlers turned their horses around and headed back down to the valley. Sam watched them go, then slanted his gaze away to watch the women building cook-fires and preparing food, and the children, more resilient than anyone ever gave them credit for, racing back and forth in some mad, frivolous game.

And then he heard it.

Hammering.

The sound of rebuilding.

Already.

"An' then some, Mrs Minto," he muttered again. "An' then some."

He sensed Matt's eyes on his profile and turned around to face him. Matt said, "You ready then, Sam?"

"I'm ready."

"Then let's go."

They turned their own mounts around and sent them up the slope and into the trees, away from the Spruce Valley settlement.

"'Course," Sam said expansively, "them Easterners're not out of the woods yet. They's Arapaho not so very far from here. Shoshone an' maybe Crow, too. Could be they still need someone to wet-nurse 'em."

Slightly taken aback, Matt said, "You're not by any chance suggesting that we turn around and go extend our visit with 'em, are you, Sam?"

Sam reached behind him and fondled Mitzi's head with his free hand. "I'm sayin' that I'm tired, Matt. Tired an' hungry. An' I'm kinda curious to see just how long I can last without a cigar."

Matt's smile was big. "Then what're we waiting for?" he asked.

A couple of minutes later two riders emerged from the timber and sent their animals down the southeastern slope at a gallop, waving their hats high above their heads to attract the attention of the people below.

Sam's raised voice filled the air. "Hello, the camp!"

And down there, in that charred valley where against all the odds, hope and optimism still thrived, settler after settler began to look up from his or her chores, recognise the not-so-newcomers and urge them on with a wave and a word, a few of them yelling in their jubilation, "*Come ahead an' welcome!*"

THE END

Other titles in the
Linford Western Library:

TOP HAND
Wade Everett

The Broken T was big. But no ranch is big enough to let a man hide from himself.

GUN WOLVES OF LOBO BASIN
Lee Floren

The Feud was a blood debt. When Smoke Talbot found the outlaws who gunned down his folks he aimed to nail their hide to the barn door.

SHOTGUN SHARKEY
Marshall Grover

The westbound coach carrying the indomitable Larry and Stretch headed for a shooting showdown.

FIGHTING RAMROD
Charles N. Heckelmann

Most men would have cut their losses, but Frazer counted the bullets in his guns and said he'd soak the range in blood before he'd give up another inch of what was his.

LONE GUN
Eric Allen

Smoke Blackbird had been away too long. The Lequires had seized the Blackbird farm, forcing the Indians and settlers off, and no one seemed willing to fight! He had to fight alone.

THE THIRD RIDER
Barry Cord

Mel Rawlins wasn't going to let anything stand in his way. His father was murdered, his two brothers gone. Now Mel rode for vengeance.

ARIZONA DRIFTERS
W. C. Tuttle

When drifting Dutton and Lonnie Steelman decide to become partners they find that they have a common enemy in the formidable Thurston brothers.

TOMBSTONE
Matt Braun

Wells Fargo paid Luke Starbuck to outgun the silver-thieving stagecoach gang at Tombstone. Before long Luke can see the only thing bearing fruit in this eldorado will be the gallows tree.

HIGH BORDER RIDERS
Lee Floren

Buckshot McKee and Tortilla Joe cut the trail of a border tough who was running Mexican beef into Texas. They stopped the smuggler in his tracks.

BRETT RANDALL, GAMBLER
E. B. Mann

Larry Day had the choice of running away from the law or of assuming a dead man's place. No matter what he decided he was bound to end up dead.

THE GUNSHARP
William R. Cox

The Eggerleys weren't very smart. They trained their sights on Will Carney and Arizona's biggest blood bath began.

THE DEPUTY OF SAN RIANO
Lawrence A. Keating and
Al. P. Nelson

When a man fell dead from his horse, Ed Grant was spotted riding away from the scene. The deputy sheriff rode out after him and came up against everything from gunfire to dynamite.

FARGO: MASSACRE RIVER
John Benteen

The ambushers up ahead had now blocked the road. Fargo's convoy was a jumble, a perfect target for the insurgents' weapons!

SUNDANCE: DEATH IN THE LAVA
John Benteen

The Modoc's captured the wagon train and its cargo of gold. But now the halfbreed they called Sundance was going after it . . .

HARSH RECKONING
Phil Ketchum

Five years of keeping himself alive in a brutal prison had made Brand tough and careless about who he gunned down . . .

FARGO: PANAMA GOLD
John Benteen

With foreign money behind him, Buckner was going to destroy the Panama Canal before it could be completed. Fargo's job was to stop Buckner.

FARGO:
THE SHARPSHOOTERS
John Benteen

The Canfield clan, thirty strong were raising hell in Texas. Fargo was tough enough to hold his own against the whole clan.

PISTOL LAW
Paul Evan Lehman

Lance Jones came back to Mustang for just one thing — revenge! Revenge on the people who had him thrown in jail.

HELL RIDERS
Steve Mensing

Wade Walker's kid brother, Duane, was locked up in the Silver City jail facing a rope at dawn. Wade was a ruthless outlaw, but he was smart, and he had vowed to have his brother out of jail before morning!

DESERT OF THE DAMNED
Nelson Nye

The law was after him for the murder of a marshal — a murder he didn't commit. Breen was after him for revenge — and Breen wouldn't stop at anything . . . blackmail, a frameup . . . or murder.

DAY OF THE COMANCHEROS
Steven C. Lawrence

Their very name struck terror into men's hearts — the Comancheros, a savage army of cutthroats who swept across Texas, leaving behind a bloodstained trail of robbery and murder.

SUNDANCE: SILENT ENEMY
John Benteen

A lone crazed Cheyenne was on a personal war path. They needed to pit one man against one crazed Indian. That man was Sundance.

LASSITER
Jack Slade

Lassiter wasn't the kind of man to listen to reason. Cross him once and he'll hold a grudge for years to come — if he let you live that long.

LAST STAGE TO GOMORRAH
Barry Cord

Jeff Carter, tough ex-riverboat gambler, now had himself a horse ranch that kept him free from gunfights and card games. Until Sturvesant of Wells Fargo showed up.

McALLISTER ON THE COMANCHE CROSSING
Matt Chisholm

The Comanche, McAllister owes them a life — and the trail is soaked with the blood of the men who had tried to outrun them before.

QUICK-TRIGGER COUNTRY
Clem Colt

Turkey Red hooked up with Curly Bill Graham's outlaw crew. But wholesale murder was out of Turk's line, so when range war flared he bucked the whole border gang alone . . .

CAMPAIGNING
Jim Miller

Ambushed on the Santa Fe trail, Sean Callahan is saved by two Indian strangers. But there'll be more lead and arrows flying before the band join Kit Carson against the Comanches.

GUNSLINGER'S RANGE
Jackson Cole

Three escaped convicts are out for revenge. They won't rest until they put a bullet through the head of the dirty snake who locked them behind bars.

RUSTLER'S TRAIL
Lee Floren

Jim Carlin knew he would have to stand up and fight because he had staked his claim right in the middle of Big Ike Outland's best grass.

THE TRUTH ABOUT SNAKE RIDGE
Marshall Grover

The troubleshooters came to San Cristobal to help the needy. For Larry and Stretch the turmoil began with a brawl and then an ambush.

WOLF DOG RANGE
Lee Floren

Will Ardery would stop at nothing, unless something stopped him first — like a bullet from Pete Manly's gun.

DEVIL'S DINERO
Marshall Grover

Plagued by remorse, a rich old reprobate hired the Texas Trouble-shooters to deliver a fortune in greenbacks to each of his victims.

GUNS OF FURY
Ernest Haycox

Dane Starr, alias Dan Smith, wanted to close the door on his past and hang up his guns, but people wouldn't let him.